T0153098

UPRIGHT
BEASTS

UPRIGHT BEASTS

STORIES ▌ LINCOLN MICHEL

 COFFEE HOUSE PRESS ▪ 2015

Coffee House Press books are available to the trade through our primary distributor, Consortium Book Sales & Distribution, cbsd.com or (800) 283-3572. For personal orders, catalogs, or other information, write to: info@coffeehousepress.org. Coffee House Press is a nonprofit literary publishing house. Support from private foundations, corporate giving programs, government programs, and generous individuals helps make the publication of our books possible. We gratefully acknowledge their support in detail in the back of this book. Visit us at coffeehousepress.org.

LIBRARY OF CONGRESS CIP INFORMATION

Michel, Lincoln.
[Short Stories. Selections]
Upright beasts : stories / Lincoln Michel.
pages cm
ISBN 978-1-56689-418-0 (paperback)
I. Title.
PS3613.I34515A6 2015
813'6—dc23

PRINTED IN THE UNITED STATES
FIRST EDITION | FIRST PRINTING

Acknowledgments

Some of these stories appeared in the following journals: "Our Education" in Electric Literature's *Recommended Reading*; "If It Were Anyone Else" in *NOON* and *Pushcart Prize XXXIX*; "The River Trick" in *Unstuck*; "Little Girls by the Side of the Pool" in *Hobart*; "Almost Recess" as "The New Game" in *Everyday Genius*; "Our New Neighborhood" in *Watchlist: 32 Short Stories by Persons of Interest* (OR Books); "Filling Pools" in *BOMB Magazine*; "Hike" in the *Collagist*; "The Deer in Virginia" as "The Deer of Virginia" in the *Oxford American*; "Halfway Home to Somewhere Else" in *Connu*; "What You Need to Know about the Weathervane" in the *Harvard Advocate*; "Lawn Dad" in *Midnight Breakfast*; "The Soldier" in *PANK*; "The Head Bodyguard Holds His Head in His Hands" in *Indiana Review*; "The Mayor's Plan" in *Mid-American Review*; "Routine" in *Monkeybicycle*; "Everybody Who's Anybody" in *New Orleans Review*; "What We Have Surmised about the John Adams Incarnation" as "John Adams" in *Forty-Four Stories about Our Forty-Four Presidents* (Melville House); "Getting There Nonetheless" in *Story*; and "A Note on the Type" in *elimae*.

For the abyss. Thanks for always gazing back.

CONTENTS

UPRIGHT BEASTS

NORTH AMERICAN MAMMALS

FAMILIAR CREATURES

UPRIGHT BEASTS

OUR EDUCATION

Time passes unexpectedly or, perhaps, inexactly at the school. It's hard to remember what semester we're in. Several of the clocks still operate, but none of them agree on the time. Construction paper murals obscure the windows. Consequently, the sun rises and falls in complete ignorance of those of us attending the school. Many of us participated in the decorations in some lost point of childhood. A few of us still have dried glue underneath our fingernails.

In the room I sit in now, the windows are covered with a glitter-and-glue reenactment of the colonization of Roanoke by Sir Walter Raleigh. Outside the window, who knows?

In my spare time, I write notes for an assignment on the state of my education. I've always believed that I was destined for somewhere better. In my hidden heart, I hold hope that my essay is the key to my escape.

My classmates laugh at me, even my second-closest friend.

"You'll never turn this in," he says, grabbing my notebook. "There will never be anyone to accept it!"

"Leave him alone," Beanpole Paula says.

"Of course you defend him," he says, winking at her from beneath his self-cropped hair.

Beanpole Paula gives my second-closest friend a sharp shove. His shirt bears the logo of a rock band I've never heard. When he smiles, I see his braces are discolored from vending machine candy. What's his name? Either Tommy or Timmy.

Obviously we no longer learn anything, or, perhaps more accurately, we learn many things, but not the things we were meant to learn. We learn about love and pain and friendship. A few of us even learn about fornication, mostly from afar (twice I've snuck behind the bleachers with Carmichael, a small and sickly boy, to watch the more muscular students tear off each other's pit-stained gym uniforms). History, mathematics, and biology are subjects lost to another time. Most of our textbooks have been repurposed for fuel. There is an ongoing fire in the back corner of the cafeteria.

I myself only own two books, novels long past their stamped due dates, which I keep tucked underneath spare clothes in the back of my locker.

Much of our hushed hallway discussion concerns the teachers. Surrounded by the pale orange lockers, we utter nasty words. We whisper out of habit. There are no teachers to overhear us. The teachers are all dead. Or else they are disintegrated. Or in hiding (but from whom? from us?). All that is known is that the teachers have disappeared, and the teachers' lounge is barricaded from the inside.

After the lunch bell, I hurry back to the front hallway with Beanpole Paula. We have an armload of chicken sandwiches, pockets filled with fries.

"That was close," she says. We slap hands in celebration.

Paula is almost six feet tall and walks with her back hunched over. I find her awkwardness endearing. She is currently my closest friend. We know our arrangement might end tomorrow, so when we smile at each other, there is a conspiracy in the air.

"We make a good team," Paula says, pressing a sandwich to her mouth with both hands. "Let's always stick together."

Then Timmy or Tommy interrupts us, rounding the corner with a half-eaten pizza slice.

Randal, two years our senior, maintains that the disappearance of the teachers is a victory for the students.

"This school only ever existed to beat us down and prepare us for a world in which we were powerless. Homework is indoctrination. Education is a cog in the machine of the ruling class."

Tommy (or Timmy) cheers him on enthusiastically. "What can you learn from teachers and tests? They're old fogies with old ideas that fossilize your brain."

Beanpole Paula and Carmichael, on the other hand, are distraught over these developments.

"What if the teachers have gone in search of better students?" Paula says. "What if we have been left behind?"

Despite beckoning from both sides, I don't enter the debate. I cannot say what the lack of faculty means. But if the teachers do return, I need to be ready with my paper. I want to believe that if they come back, I will be chosen to graduate to a better place.

I keep the assignment folded in my back pocket. I don't remember when I received it, but it's my strongest proof that our teachers are coming back. The sheet of paper says, *In your own words: a) what is the goal of your education, and b) how far are you, in your mind, to achieving this goal?*

The top left corner lists the period, classroom number, and teacher from whom the assignment supposedly came. *Second period, room 17, Ms. Lispector.* I hold the assignment close to my face and try to remember her. I see an older woman with dyed black hair and a blue ankle-length dress, but the image is as blurry as a bigfoot photo.

"Do you like her?"

Beanpole Paula's eyes follow mine as they survey the globe-like behind of Lydia Pill.

"I don't even know her," I say.

"That wasn't the question."

In my memories, Lydia and I sat next to each other in sex ed. We were paired up for several projects. Now, as I watch her body cross the room, my mind conjures up the faded diagrams and illustrations on the pull-down posters in room 201. I try to visualize those impossible organs hiding behind her clothes. I begin to sweat.

Lydia is walking hand in hand with Clint Bulger. Bulger is, or I suppose I should say was, the captain of the football team. We're most afraid of Bulger and the other jocks, who, having cordoned off the basketball courts and adjacent locker rooms, have access to softball bats and hockey sticks.

"I don't know," I say, watching them stroll by without even looking at us. Lydia's golden hair sways between her shoulder blades in a thick ponytail.

"I knew it," Paula says loudly. She grabs her own hair. "I know everything. I have terrible powers."

"What's wrong?" I say, turning to Paula. She looks very sad. I place a hand on her shoulder to comfort her. Then her forehead wrinkles, and I realize that she isn't sad. She is angry. She twists my arm around my back and pushes me off the radiator. I struggle, but Paula has leverage and pins me to the linoleum with her long limbs.

"You think you'll be the only one rewarded. I can see into the future, and I know exactly what horrible tragedy you're heading toward." Her voice is very loud now. "While you, you can't even see what's in front of your own nose!"

Through the veil of Paula's brown hair, I watch Lydia and Bulger disappear up the staircase.

One quirk of the school is the teachers' lounge, which sits in the middle of the circular cafeteria. The school is three stories tall, and the lounge is a large cylindrical structure at its center. The lounge is constructed from tinted windows. This dark glass faces the clear windows of the classrooms with a twelve-foot gap between them.

Most of the students, even those who are convinced the teachers have vanished, find the teachers' lounge eerie. Consequently, only the least popular and most powerless of the cliques—the dweebs, the dorks, and the dinguses—occupy any of the classrooms facing the lounge. The rest of us only enter those rooms to scavenge for supplies, and even then we hoist our T-shirts above our noses to mask our identities.

Perhaps it's inaccurate to call this structure the teachers' lounge. This is merely our assumption. Nothing about it, from the outside, appears particularly lounge-like. Its doors are bolted shut, and it's the only area—other than the outside, of course—that is inaccessible to us. Any surviving teachers must be inside if they remain in the school. We have searched all other rooms and found no bodies, living or dead.

While holding a pile of reheated tater tots in the scoop of my shirt, I run into Lydia as I round the curve of the lounge. She is sitting on a cafeteria table and drinking a diet soda. When we collide, the tater tots scatter and bounce off the black glass.

"Whoops!" she says. I watch her mouth as she speaks. Her lips are plump and appealing. I haven't yet kissed a girl's lips. I've only had Beanpole Paula's touch my cheeks.

"I'm sorry," I say. I get on my knees to sweep up the brown barrels rolling in the dust.

"Don't worry about it." She bends down in front of me, her padded breasts at the exact same level as my eyes. She is wearing lavender deodorant. The smell wraps around me, and I begin to feel dizzy.

"Do you remember me? We were in health together, maybe biology too."

"Oh yeah," she says. "You used to draw those funny pictures on desks of the teachers being eaten by monsters, right?" She laughs, and I laugh with her. "I'd almost forgotten about that. It was so long ago it seems like a dream."

I look into her eyes as her hands place the tots in mine.

"What the fuck are you two doing on the floor?" yells Clint Bulger, emerging from the kitchen with a plate of fries.

I don't believe Bulger suspects anything, but he has begun squinting at me when we use adjacent urinals in the boys' room.

Sneaking out of an algebra classroom, I run into Beanpole Paula and Timmy (I have decided that this is indeed his name). They're whispering by a corkboard with sign-ups for clubs that no longer meet. With one hand, Timmy strokes Paula's improbably thin forearms.

"I didn't see you there," Paula says, backing away suddenly from Timmy.

Timmy says nothing, only shifts his eyes between Paula and me.

• • •

I've decided I can no longer allow my friends to be aware of my assignment. I have to write in a boys' room stall while moaning and feigning stomach problems. I may have to abandon the paper altogether. The faction that hates our missing teachers grows stronger every day. I don't want to arouse any suspicion. It's best to blend in.

"How's your paper coming along?" Tommy (I was mistaken before) says to me. He is leaning against the lockers and drumming on his knees.

"What paper? I got rid of that a while ago," I say loudly. "I used a Bunsen burner from the biology closet."

"Bunsen burner? That sounds like a test term. Are you reading old tests?" Tommy smirks.

I have been downgraded out of his closest circle of friends.

I think most of us believe that time doesn't really exist outside the school. Or at least we act as if it doesn't. That is to say, we know there was life before the school, in theory, and that there will be life after the school, if we can ever get out. But the time that passes here is the immediate time, and the problems of our life in the school are the problems that seem most real to us. Take, for example, my situation with Lydia. I would likely trade years of my future for her soft lips underneath the bleachers today.

Beliefs evolve. Many of the students who only yesterday hated our teachers now deny they ever existed. Tommy angrily tells us that no teachers ever lived, and if they did, they certainly didn't teach. They only watched us and recorded our actions and doled out punishments or rewards while laughing from inside the dark lounge.

"But I remember the lessons," Carmichael says meekly. "I can still smell the eraser dust and hear the squeak of chalk."

Tommy hooks Carmichael's neck with one arm and mercilessly digs his knuckles into his scalp with the other. The rest of us watch with our convictions hidden inside.

There were teachers once. There was Mrs. Blackwood, Mr. Cupp, Ms. Urrutia, Mr. and Mrs. Slaughter, Ms. Lispector, Mr. Gunten, Coach Neck, Coach Cuthbert, Principal Always, at least two nurses, several guidance counselors, and other assorted faculty members and school staff whose names I have forgotten.

This is something I still believe.

Tensions are becoming increasingly apparent in our group. Carmichael and others are rebelling at Tommy's ascendency. Beanpole Paula tries to broker peace. I fear for the worst.

I must confess that I can no longer remember the specifics of any teacher. Their faces are Rorschach blots in my mind.

In the early days, when we were all still close, I scavenged with Paula and Tommy. We found objects that are hard to explain: cold cups of coffee, stacks of gold stickers, a woman's shoe stained with Wite-Out. Is it possible these articles aren't real? That they were fabricated by some unknown force? (The force inside the dark lounge?) Did we students, in our weakness, fabricate whole memories from these scattered, pointless items?

Even these few remains are disappearing. Roving bands scour the old classrooms and destroy all heretical items on the orders of Bulger.

Did I forget to mention that Bulger has recently, through a series of calculated attacks and negotiations, consolidated power among the school groups? All decisions about the school must now go through him. He holds court in the equipment room, surrounded by balls and sticks.

I'm not sure what is happening with Paula. She does not confide in me anymore. She won't talk to me alone, only in our group, and even then Tommy will tug at her elbow if it's for more than a sentence.

"I've got to go," she says, looking at the floor.

Her change in habits has led to odd feelings in my stomach. I used to think of Paula as an old friend, no different from Carmichael, Jamal, or anyone else. But now that she is no longer close to me, I begin to regard her in a new light.

How did I, before, miss the delicate shine of her brown hair or the way her eyes feel so joyful even when they are full of sorrow?

There has been a significant development. Timmy Thomas (herein lies the source of my confusion) and Jamal have discovered camouflaged cables running from the teachers' lounge. The cables are hidden beneath the carpet and disguised as school spirit decorations running up the pipes. When the cables reach the ceiling, they blossom out through various vents and openings.

This information was turned over to Clint Bulger, who praised Timmy and Jamal for their service. I always knew that Timmy wanted to be a part of Bulger's crowd, and had only settled for us when he was spurned. Now Bulger has promoted them to official members of his clique.

We're not sure where the cables lead. There are whispers that the teachers are still watching us through hidden cameras. That one day soon they will surface and either reward or punish us for our actions. The old beliefs reemerge.

Bulger is angered by these rumors. He believes they give hope to radical elements.

"Cut them," he orders. "Cut them all."

"Paula?"

"Oh, I didn't see you there."

"I was waiting for you. I have things I have to tell you. Things about you and about me. Weird things, wobbly feelings in my chest that I've started to discover."

"Oh no, not now! It's too late now."

Two tears begin to form in the corners of her lovely eyes.

Disaster! My assignment on the state of our education has been found. I'm dragged through the coldly lit hallways by two ex-linebackers. Although I'd stopped working on the essay a long time ago, I couldn't destroy it. There was some small hope glimmering in the back of my mind.

The ex-linebackers toss me on the equipment room floor. Clint Bulger sits on the coach's chair. To the right, Timmy Thomas whispers into his ear. To the left, Lydia flips the pages of a magazine with her delicate fingers. She doesn't even look down at me. Why had I ever imagined the possibility of a connection between us?

In front of me lie the crumpled pages of my assignment and an old teacher's tie that I had saved from destruction.

"What do you have to say about all this?" Bulger bellows.

"How did you get my locker combination?"

Timmy chuckles. "Did you think I'd forget about your precious essay?"

"You know that worship of the false teachers is forbidden," Bulger says. He stands up, holding an aluminum baseball bat as his staff. He picks up one page of my essay and smooths it out.

"The goal of our education is to afford us the skills needed to graduate and pursue further education at greater institutions." He snorts. "What does that even mean? That our education never ends? That we're trapped in a hell of infinite schools?" He crumples the page back up and tosses it on the floor.

"The concept of the teachers is absurd. What kind of teacher would leave their students? Such a teacher would be no teacher at all. So, we must conclude that the teachers are a false tale that students tell themselves to avoid facing the real struggles in their lives. They're a myth, and a harmful one."

"If that's true," I say, getting to my knees, "then who do you think is in the black lounge?"

"Silence!" Timmy yells.

Bulger merely laughs.

I'm being held in the equipment cage. My guard passes me Gatorade and granola bars through the gaps. Clint Bulger comes to see me, to ask if I repent. I say nothing.

"You know," he says, sitting on a kickball, "you look very familiar to me."

"Yes!" I say, hoping to appeal to his sense of fraternity. I crawl closer to the wire grid. "We used to ride the bus together. We both sat in the back row. We were almost friends."

"No," Bulger says. He sighs and rises. "You still don't understand. There never was any bus."

I'm napping on a pile of gym mats when I hear a voice softly say my name.

"They let me see you," Beanpole Paula says. "I said I'd reason with you."

She slips me a chocolate chip cookie through the gap. Her hand brushes mine as she does.

"Thanks," I say.

Paula is silent as I take a bite.

"Do you really want to leave the school so badly?"

"I could stay," I say, leaning against the cage. "I could stay with you."

She gives me a look that feels as if it is traveling to me from some vast, cold distance. Then she turns her head away.

"I'm with Timmy now. You know that."

"I don't know what's true and what's false. I only believe there must be a better, more important place than this."

"Then I hope you find it," Paula says. She starts to say something else, but instead turns away with her mouth partly ajar.

Past crushes, friends, rivals, and strangers alike jeer and shout as I'm dragged through the hallway. My head pulses as it hits the tile floor. A little stream of blood trickles out of my nose. When I raise my head, I see the dark teachers' lounge towering over me.

"This heretical loser has turned his back on all of us," Bulger shouts. The student body has assembled on the different floors overlooking the cafeteria. They are silent and watching. "But we aren't unreasonable people. In fact, we want to give him a choice. He may repent and return to his clique, or he may live for the rest of his days inside his sacred lounge."

The shouts of the students fall around me. I look up at the different faces staring down. Some are sympathetic, some seem angry, but most are simply bored. The most venomous face belongs to Timmy. He spits on the tile floor.

Paula is next to him, and her eyes are red. I look into them, hoping, perhaps, for some sign. I think that maybe she will leap forward and block the entrance, telling the whole school of our love. But she doesn't move. She looks back at me with resignation, as if she is reminiscing about those lost, carefree recesses spent swinging together on the monkey bars.

I turn back to the looming walls of the lounge.

"If he has nothing to say, so be it," Bulger says. "Boys, open."

The ex-linebackers jam crowbars into the door of the black lounge. It takes four of them to finally swing it open with a loud crack. The inside is the blackest black I have ever seen. As the doors are pulled open, everything turns silent. I can no longer hear the heckling or shouts of my fellow students. My friends and enemies fade away behind me. The only thing before me is the darkness of the lounge.

I'm on my knees in front of the doorway, holding my assignment out in my hand.

IF IT WERE ANYONE ELSE

A bald man buddied up to me in the elevator, but he was no buddy of mine. He was much older than me, yet more or less exactly as tall, not counting my hair. He was holding a brown paper bag over his crotch.

"Does this go all the way to the roof?"

I made a big show of putting my newspaper down and turning my head. "What the hell do I know about the roof? What would I do all the way up there?"

We stood still as we moved up the building.

"Just a friendly question." He licked the bottom of his mustache with the tip of his tongue. "Hey, do you like candy beans?"

There was no one else on the elevator, and then the doors opened and a woman in a green pantsuit stepped in. She looked at us and moved to the other corner.

"Who doesn't?" I hissed.

The man opened his paper bag and dug around. He offered me an assortment in his palm. I took four of the red and six of the purple.

I got out two-thirds of the way up. The building I worked in was very tall, more or less exactly as tall as the tallest building in that part of the city, not counting the antenna. I often forgot how tall the building was because I kept the office blinds half-closed. If I opened them, I would get unnerved by the eye-level workers looking back at me from the building across the street.

My company occupied four floors of the building, but they weren't consecutive. Between the lowest floor we owned and the third-highest floor we owned, there was a snack company. I had been working at my company for some time. I now worked on the top floor of the floors we owned, but I had worked on the lowest floor, and also the floor above the snack company. I had never worked on the floor that was two floors above the snack company and one floor below my current floor.

The snack company often had sample bowls set up for new products they were testing. I liked to go down there and unwrap a few when I could get away for a bit.

The older bald man was sitting in a red leather chair near the elevator. He turned and smiled up at me as I pressed the down button.

"How was the roof?" I said. "Did you find what you were looking for?"

"Oh, I couldn't get all the way to the top. I got pretty close though. It was real nice, even not quite at the top. You could see the park and everything." He was nodding agreeably.

"Do you have business on this floor? Those red chairs are for people who have business on this floor." We had four red leather chairs around a coffee table in the hallway. There was also a tall, thin plant that I was pretty sure was plastic.

The man looked up at me with a cautious smile.

I looked at him in his ugly, unbuttoned suit. The top of his head shone under the fluorescent light. My face must have shown my disgust.

"Okay," he said with an exaggerated frown. "I get it. You've got work to do. Maybe some other time."

I didn't live in the city proper; I lived in one of the outer boroughs. You couldn't see it from my office window, on account of all the tall buildings. The buildings were much shorter in my borough.

I spent a lot of time traveling over and under water. There were many bridges and tunnels connecting my borough and the city. I didn't like going through the tunnels. Sometimes the subway would stop deep underground, and I'd close my eyes and try to think of something other than water rushing in and drowning everyone in the car.

I'd taken the blue bridge on the subway to get to work. After work, I walked back along the brown bridge. It was a nice day, and the bridge was crammed with people. There were lots of children throwing scraps of food over the railing and down into the water.

About halfway across the bridge, I thought I saw the bald man, and I turned quickly and tried to duck. A biker was biking past me and shouted out, "You're going to kill everyone!" He started wobbling but didn't tip over. A few people yelled at the biker while he was yelling at me.

I stayed crouching for a few moments. I could see the cars whizzing by beneath me through the slats. There were millions of people in the city, but you just never knew.

I thought I saw the bald man again that evening. The man I saw was shouting in my direction from up the street, but he had a fedora pulled down low on his head, so I wasn't sure.

I stepped into a new cookie shop that had opened on my corner. Before that, it had been a macaron shop, and, when I had first moved in, a cupcake shop. But it had originally been a cookie shop. Things always came around like that in this part of the city.

I was wrong about the man on the street. He must have been shouting at a cab. The bald man I'd been ducking was inside the cookie shop with a whole stack and a two-thirds empty glass of milk.

"Wow," he said. He jumped out of his chair. "Now this is a coincidence. This has to mean something, right?"

I thought about leaving, going to the brownie shop next door, but I didn't want him to think he had that kind of power over me.

He walked up beside me at the counter. "Hey buddy, I got an idea. Do you like ballgames?"

The woman at the counter was asking for my order. Her eyeballs rolled in their sockets.

"Sure," I said. "Everyone likes ballgames."

"Let's go to the ballgame. You and me. Just two guys watching a ballgame. What's wrong with that? I got an extra ticket."

I didn't look at him, but I felt his hand on my shoulder. I could tell he was going to keep bothering me. He was like a stray mangy dog I'd unthinkingly fed scraps to.

"Just this once," I sighed. "One ballgame."

The man slapped his hands together and walked toward the door.

"Not now. I want to finish my snack. I came here to have a snack," I said.

The man had the door open, and he started to close it. "We'll miss the first inning," he said. He looked surprisingly annoyed, but then he cheered up. "That's okay. The team never gets going until the second or third. Okay. Yeah. I'll be sitting over there until you're done."

The man led me to a damp parking garage deep underground and unlocked the doors to a beige sedan. He looked at me and started to say something, but he stopped himself. He faced forward and turned on the ignition.

"Let's just take it slow. One day at a time," he said.

"Sure, whatever you say."

We drove up the slanted cement. I stared ahead.

"I only thought we could go to a nice ballgame. Do you like rock 'n' roll? Let's listen to some rock 'n' roll." At first we were still a few floors too far underground. Then the static broke into clear guitars as we drove onto the street.

There were bits of trash all over the floor of the car, old snack wrappers and the like. "This is a pigsty. Do you live in here? How old is this car, anyway? It still has a tape player. They don't even make tapes anymore!"

His face and head started to turn a reddish color, and his knuckles turned white on the steering wheel. I saw his chapped lips count quietly down from ten. "What do you think about our bullpen?" he said after a minute. He tried to smile. "Let's talk about the bullpen."

The ballpark was in yet another borough. The road was flat all the way there. It was a brand-new ballpark that had cost the team and the city a lot of money. It was large and open. The breeze could come in and out, and there were all sorts of food and snacks being sold, even sushi. I went to this ballpark pretty frequently with clients. I never knew where my company's seats would be. Sometimes the clients and I were way at the top, overhanging the field. Other times, we were down low, almost level with the players.

When we pulled up, there were no other cars in the parking lot. There was no one walking up and down the stadium. It was just the quiet and the man and me in a dirty old car.

He turned off the gas and hung his bare head. "The game must be tomorrow," he said after a bit.

I gave a laugh. I reached out and calmly placed a hand on his damp, bald head. "Isn't this just perfect? You dumb schmuck! Harass me all day and take me to an abandoned ballpark."

The man got out of the car, and I got out after him. He tore off his suit jacket and rolled it into a ball. He pressed this against his mouth and yelled into it.

Gray pigeons walked around us, knocking their heads down at fossilized pizza crusts. It was quiet and peaceful.

I got up behind him and grabbed his shoulder. He dropped the jacket on the pavement.

"Hey," I said.

We were getting somewhere now.

THE RIVER TRICK

Upstairs Jack uses knives, Mrs. Murmur prefers pills, and Lloyd drops electrical appliances into his bathtub. We all have our vices. I, for one, drink heavily. I try not to on the job though, because timing is everything with suicides.

Patricia and I moved into this apartment complex four months ago. We had been having a hard time making it in the city, and after I lost my job driving subway cars, we could no longer afford the rents. It isn't so bad on the outskirts. We have a nice building made out of solid brick. There's a small garden in the back, and we can take our cats, Spick and Span, outside to dig around in the flowers. Patricia has a longer commute, but I get to work from home.

My various neighbors try to kill themselves at least twice a month. They're not very good at it. Upstairs Jack's kitchen is stocked with plastic utensils. Lloyd doesn't bother plugging in the toaster and sometimes doesn't even fill the tub. Mrs. Murmur fails to realize you can't overdose on sugar pills; the placebo effect just doesn't reach that far.

In the mornings, I saw a grapefruit in half and pour a bowl of cereal. If I can, I exercise. Twenty push-ups, twenty pull-ups, and a twenty-minute run. It's easier to remember that way. Afterwards, I check the queue from the Apartment Wellness Committee website listing the who/what/when/where. I lay out my schedule, squeeze my neighbors into their proper slots.

Of course, sometimes the clerk forgets to log an appointment, or else I sleep through my alarm and rush down the hall to find Tina Okada crumpled on the floor with a broken piece of twine around her neck, glaring angrily at me.

Mix-ups, complications; these are the inevitable kinks in the hose of human operations. Yesterday, Patricia burned my toast while talking on the phone with her sister. I understood.

It isn't anything sexual, the suicides. I feel I should make that clear. I was raised in the country, a full-fledged farm butting right up against our backyard. When I visit my family, they ask about this.

"We hear people in the city do weird things in bed," they say.

"We hear they're perverts, every last one."

"We hear of acts that aren't right to speak about in proper company."

"Well," I say, "it's a crazy world every which way you look."

But as far as I can tell, the suicides are not part of this. My customers don't seem to be in any erotic throes. I don't find them with wet latex hanging from their limp organs or flecks of fake blood dotting their exposed nipples. They're always properly dressed, with faces curled in pain, not pleasure. I know there are people who believe sex is an extension of death, but I've never experienced this. Things are what they are and not other things.

I'm not here to judge anyway. I do my job, and afterwards I live my own life. If I see my neighbors when I'm swapping my wet laundry into the dryer, I make the necessary small talk. I don't think of them lying in their bathtubs, beds, or on their living room floors. I try not to even speculate as to their reasons.

And yet. Abusive boyfriend? Failed acting career? A mother who refused to hug them as a child? It does make you wonder.

Patricia calls them "cries for help." I don't know. Sometimes it's just something to do on a Friday night.

My Fridays are fairly laid-back. I cook spaghetti with garlic bread, and after Patricia gets off work, we eat and stream a movie on TV.

Patricia and I don't make love too often these days. Our schedules are out of sync. She leaves in the morning when I'm still groggy in bed, and if we talk it's only to fight. This morning it's about the new flatscreen I bought. Something popped in the old one, and the upper left corner was turning everything green. Patricia wasn't around to discuss it. She works late hours as a cultural advisor to the mayor, deciding which artists to shake hands with at press conferences and the like. It doesn't pay as well as you'd think.

"Can't you think about us, not yourself?" she says.

"We both watch TV," I say, but she's already out the door.

I chew my grapefruit and do my push-ups. Spick claws at my calf, and Span stares out the window at the birds chirping in the trees.

Afterwards, I put on my tie and walk downstairs to Earl's apartment. It's a bright day, and the sun pours into the hallway. Earl's door is partly open.

"Earl," I say, walking in, "I'm trying a new Thai recipe and was wondering if you had any sweet paprika that I could— dear god!"

Earl is standing on the kitchen table, beer cans rolling around his feet. An extension cord has been tossed over the revolving fan. The end is tied around Earl's neck.

"What the devil are you doing?" I ask.

"I've decided to end it all," he says. "I can't just keep waiting for nature to do it for me."

"No, Earl, you can't do this! Think of your family. Think of the butcher and the barber who depend on your patronage. Think of your dogs, the happy wagging of their tails."

"Yes, there are those considerations, but is that enough? Life is so very hard."

The revolving fan twists slowly with the weight of the orange cord, pulling it tighter around Earl's neck. He's standing on the toes of his leather boots. He looks ready to drop off the table.

"Life may be hard," I say. "Yes, life might be a rash on your anus, but there are always things on the horizon to wait for. There are balloons and candy bars, if you like candy bars. There are cloudless days and bottles of sunscreen. There are many things I've forgotten about but will tell you later. And then there's love in the end, yes? The great hope? Love in the end."

Earl's face is contorted in shame. I think I see tears peeking from the edges of his eyes. "I never thought about it like that," he says.

He gets down and slips a five-dollar tip into my hand, asks me if I want some coffee. Earl is one of the ones who likes to talk afterwards. We discuss the weather, the recent home team's victory against the visiting team, politicians and the interiors of their bedrooms.

The routine varies.

In bed, Patricia tells me how the people in the city aren't happy, and the mayor is nervous. The election is only months away. The mayor spends his days shouting into the red telephone.

"Paul, you have to get me out of this one!" he says. "Stephanie, you're my spin queen. Spin it for me, baby, please!"

Patricia says she commissioned a study that reached a tentative conclusion: the people in the city feel detached from their surroundings. "More and more, people are sticking to themselves and only staring into their screens," Patricia says.

"The city is an alien thing," I say. "If it weren't for my job, I wouldn't even know my neighbors' names."

Patricia clicks off the light, and we go to sleep.

Soon the mayor creates a plan for "aesthetic interactivity" to bring people closer to their city, their home. Patricia sets up the whole thing. She orchestrates a network of cameras and projectors to display the images of the people on the street onto large screens draped between the buildings. This way, people can't help but view themselves as part of the city's ecosystem.

I don't leave my apartment much, yet I wonder how the people take it. Do they like watching themselves as they go about their chores? Do they wave and perform? Do they see their images in the sky and think of themselves as stars? Most are probably caught unaware.

At night, our cats meow out the window. The image of a young woman angrily hitting her lover with a handful of flowers is projected from the street onto a screen right outside. Autumn has begun, and leaves disrupt the picture as they fall.

With the election looming, Patricia has been called on to work longer hours. Most days I'm awoken by her clicking shut the door.

I have my regulars in the building, but people always come and go. After lunch, I have a new customer who marks herself down for razors. I make a turkey and cheddar sandwich with too much mustard and crack open a tin of tuna for the cats. I eat the sandwich as I climb the stairs to the fifth floor. When I knock no one answers.

I figure this girl doesn't know the rules, even though they were explicitly spelled out on the consent form. Either that or she got a date with a cute boy and has given up on the suicide drama.

"Fuck it," I say, and almost turn to head back to my room. Instead, I sigh and use an old debit card to jimmy the door open.

The apartment is a clean one, with blue walls and bright light pouring in through the blinds. I don't see my client anywhere. I close the door and go through the act, say, "I'm just the power man casually checking the meter." I don't hear any response.

"Daphne Bankhead?" I say. It's moments like these that remind me why this job was open and how lonely even attempting human contact can be.

Then I find her draped over the toilet with red trickling across the floor. She's wearing a green dress, and her hair is pulled back with yellow barrettes.

I rush over and lift her off the toilet. I yank off two wads of toilet paper and press them to her wrists. She gives me a little smile.

"I thought you were supposed to be here at two thirty," she says.

"You put down three."

"My bad," she says.

I lean her against the side of the bathtub and grab a washcloth to wipe away the blood. The wounds are thin slits across her wrists, although not in the right direction to finish her off. Not unless I'd left her bleeding there for a week or so. Still, the whole thing puts me on edge.

"You're not supposed to go this far with it," I say. "I'm not licensed in any medical capacity."

I look at her face, trying to decide if I've seen her in the building before. A thin sheet of sweat is making her forehead shine. I grab a handful of Band-Aids and wrap them one by one around her wrists.

"I guess I got carried away," she says. "I used to be a bit of a thespian in high school."

Outside I can hear dogs barking and cars honking by. Daphne smiles and lifts her face to mine.

I might have made a miscalculation earlier. There were certain facts I hadn't taken into consideration: the French calling the orgasm "le petite mort" or "the little death," certain theories of Freud's, autoerotic asphyxiation, and so on. Sex, which is in some sense life, is forever caught up in the struggle with death.

Daphne, with her eyes like fistfuls of diamonds, was yet another mistake.

Patricia in a blue dress. Patricia making me cucumber and cream cheese sandwiches with the crusts cut off for lunch. The cats, Spick and Span, rubbing against her leg as Patricia feeds them the crusts. Patricia with her slanted smile teaching me to dance. Walking down the street arm in arm, an old friend, "Patricia!" Patricia taking cooking lessons. The phone rings, I pick it up: "Patricia?" Patricia fed up. Patricia fed up with my fucking drinking. Patricia: "I know all about it, you asshole. I know all about that fifth-floor slut, Daphne." Patricia with a suitcase. Patricia with a large yellow suitcase at the door. The door closing. Patricia. Patricia. Patricia.

I lie in bed most nights, thinking of things.

This suicide problem is becoming a real crisis. Especially with the recent deaths (human error crops up everywhere).

I myself am dragged before a judge after Mrs. Murmur finally succeeds. I've been drinking since Patricia left, and when the alarm went off, I punched it off the bedside table. A few hours later, I stumbled into Mrs. Murmur's room, and she was turning blue, her hairdryer's power cord snug around her powdery neck. Her eyes were still open and staring at me.

The judge asks me how I let this happen after all my training.

"Training, Your Honor?"

"For your certification."

"Certification, Your Honor?"

I lose the job and am sentenced to five months of community service at the homeless shelter. It's pretty much the same gig, except it doesn't pay.

My absence doesn't stop things. Two days later, Upstairs Jack is in the hospital getting his wrists stitched up. My job is reinstated under the table.

This kind of thing is happening all over the city. People are taking matters into their own hands. The countryside seems immune to the problem, but the city is slowly falling apart. You can't even turn on a talk show without hearing competing experts shouting their different theories.

The election is looming like a wolf at the gates. The mayor has to do something. When he appears in public, he yanks his tie.

Interrupting a college football game, the mayor announces a plan that I know is Patricia's. The mayor talks about a great entrepreneur named Dr. Sam. "Dr. Sam has a stunning new product to innovate his native city," the mayor says. "He will use a series of chemicals to turn our great river into a chromatic display of the city's emotions. An algorithm will squirt the chemicals into the river based on our citizens' social media activity. It will create a mood ring flowing all around us."

Dr. Sam takes the stage wearing a lab coat over his polo and jeans.

"Imagine the innovative rainbow of our collective emotions disrupting the stagnant waters of our beloved river! Samples of the river rainbow can be purchased in-app for $29.99. City Hall will even throw in a free tote bag."

I turn off the TV and head to my mandatory community volunteering.

The whole city has gone to hell. My cereal is soggy, the citrus is sour. I get lonely. The cat, Spick, meows constantly. Patricia took Span with her, along with the computer and most of our books. She left me the flatscreen though.

The workload is unbearable as more and more people sign up. Now, when I make my rounds, I say, "You idiot! You big dumbo! Stop that, just stop it right now!"

Sometimes Daphne comes to my door. "I was wondering if you wanted to go to the ceremony."

"Which one?" I say.

"At the Remembering Day Memorial Bridge. Dr. Sam is going to perform the river trick today."

"I'll think about it."

"Then," she says, "perhaps I'll see you there."

"Perhaps." I clink the ice in my glass until she closes the door.

By the time I get there, the bridge is packed as tightly as a supermarket shelf. I sip a flask of whiskey as I listen to the recycled speeches and watch the middle school talent shows. Finally, a woman in a sparkly dress cuts the ribbon with three-foot scissors.

Everyone around me looks nervous. I look for Patricia but don't see her. Dr. Sam yanks the large lever, and the blue chemicals jump free into the river. Everyone grows silent. Several mothers hoist their babies high in the air.

We fidget and wait.

The river begins to glow a bright yellow.

There are reports that where the yellow river crashes into the sea, seagulls fly away in fear. There are reports that fish near the river's mouth leap out of the water to die on the rocks. These reports are not considered credible, and only 40 percent of people polled believe them. Still.

It should be no surprise that timelines and status updates are filled with jokes at the expense of the "yellow river," but I don't find them funny. I find the whole situation sad and take to drinking even more.

Time passes in that way it likes to pass, without you even wanting to notice. I do my job for the people who want it, but many move on to more intense experiences. Daphne moves to another city by another river. The mayor is defeated in the election by a younger man with a bigger smile. The new mayor's mood doesn't transfer to the citizens though. The river slowly turns back to its traditional brown as the chemicals drain away.

Then one day I run into Patricia as I'm walking alongside the river looking to buy some tomatoes. She looks a bit older and a bit sadder.

"Hello," she says.

"Long time," I say.

We walk together up the riverside, reminiscing. We talk for a long time about this and that. Up on the bridge, I can see many people with wide-open eyes. I can almost make out the fear in those eyes, and the tears glinting in the sun. The people carry armfuls of bricks or old appliances to weigh them down. I see Earl and Upstairs Jack standing on the rail. Earl gives me an embarrassed wave.

"Can't we just start over?" I ask Patricia.

"Will you drink less?"

"I could hide it better."

"Will there be children?"

"Two of them. The patter of their little feet will keep us awake all night."

A policewoman comes up and tells us to move along. "Nothing to see here," she says. "Not even that stuff you're looking at."

Patricia and I walk across the road. Her hand brushes mine.

One by one the people on the bridge hurtle into the cold waters, their arms wrapped around microwaves and cordless vacuums. They fall straighter than I ever thought possible.

"Will there be love?"

"That I can't promise," I say, "but we can try to fight our way through it together."

And perhaps seconds later, the people come rocketing back to the surface, having abandoned their appliances. They bob and gasp. And maybe they will have found something down there while starving for air. On the surface, they will seek each other out and cling tightly, saying, "This is what I need. This is what I've been waiting for."

I'm not sure. Patricia and I have walked too far away to see.

LITTLE GIRLS BY THE SIDE OF THE POOL

"Did you see what Suzy did when her father tossed her into the air?"

"No, I was looking at Jimmy."

"She screamed. She screamed like a little piglet right until she hit the water."

"My father is *really* good at tossing me into the water."

"Yes, *my* father can toss me so high I'm afraid I'll never come down."

"My father once threw me like ten feet out of the water, and I did two cartwheels in the air before splashing."

"My father once tossed me so high into the air that I was at eye level with the top of a tall tree, and in that tree was a bird, and that bird unfurled its wings and looked at me in a loving way, like a sister."

"When I see you and your father in the pool, he is not tossing you or throwing you. Rather, he is holding you under the water, and you are trying to swim between his legs to twist him up, or else clawing his knees, trying to reach the air."

"Yes. My father is good at tossing, but he is also good at holding."

"Does he hold you only in the water?"

"No. Many places. Sometimes I will walk into a room and his hand, lying on the armrest of his chair, will begin to twitch."

"I don't think I like your father."

"I hate *all* fathers. It is the way they touch you."

"Their hands are swollen. When you are born, they can carry you in their palm. You grow older and taller, and yet their hands never shrink. When one wraps around your shoulder, the weight immobilizes you."

"And those hands, they can take control of you. You will be standing in the doorway to the kitchen, and on the kitchen table is something wretched, some burnt meat, and in the chair at the table is someone wretched, a boy that has been invited over to talk to you, but whom you already talk to in school and despise. Your mother has dressed you up too, in some frilly dress that would look stupid even on a doll, and you are standing in the doorframe about to retreat, to flee back to your room, where you cannot see or smell any of the wretched things in the kitchen, but as you are about to turn, the hand of your father appears on your shoulder, and it moves through you, it pilots you, and suddenly you are walking into the kitchen even though you didn't want to go into the kitchen—or maybe it is the dentist's or a therapist's office or piano lessons—and the hand just appears there and wills you to enter without your father even speaking, wills itself over the will of your own bones, forcing you into the room even though the hand itself does not move, does not even flinch."

". . ."

"But even so, those are also the hands that send you cartwheeling through the air above a body of water the exact color of the bottom of a Bomb Pop."

"My father is not the only one who tosses me out of the water."

"Oh? And who tosses you? Your filthy brothers?"

"Yes, my brothers. Tossing me together, one on each side, a leg and arm held in the hands of one, the other leg and other arm gripped in the fists of the other. They look at each other and count to a number while swinging me. When they reach the number, they release me. I never know what the number will be. That is part of the game. They tell me a number, but the number they tell me is never the number that prompts my release."

"Brothers are even worse than fathers. Brothers are fathers in training. They carry a father around in their bellies, and the beard of this father irritates the walls of their stomachs. This is the reason they are angry, all the time, when they see you."

"I *have* noticed their hands twitching in a familiar way."

"They are not the same hands as the hands of fathers, but they share the same hardness."

"Well, my father and my brothers are not the only ones who toss me out of the water. Sometimes I will wait until the lifeguards rotate shifts, and when Jimmy gets his turn to take a break, he will slide off his white tank top and pull off his red whistle. When I see him do this, I slip into the water. I fill my lungs with as much air as I can and swim underwater from the deep end to the shallow end where Jimmy will be standing, leaning against the wall of the pool, really, when I emerge. He does not say anything, and I cannot look him in the eye. I look down at his stomach. The sun reflects off the mix of water and sunscreen on his chest in a way that hurts my eyes, yet makes me feel protected."

"And then he tosses you out of the water?"

"Sometimes. If I open my eyes wide enough."

"He tosses you away."

" . . . "

" . . . "

"I can only see his eyes vaguely behind the sunglasses. They are like two beautiful fish in the depths of a muddy lake."

"They are different eyes when the sunglasses are off."

"How do you know?"

"Sometimes Jimmy takes me out of the water to a dark place behind the bushes, and he takes off his sunglasses with one hand while the other hand approaches me."

"And these are the eyes you hate? The eyes that thin to the edge of a knife when he approaches?"

"No, it's as if his eyes are clouds that have emptied themselves of rain."

"Like a villain? Like some foreign villain in a cartoon? His left hand stroking his thin early pubescent mustache, his right held high in anger?"

"No, it isn't like that at all."

"The way his eyes grab hold of you at the same time his hands do? The way his fingers tear into your shoulder blades as his eyes move closer—"

"No. Jimmy's hands go other places."

"Those cold, dead eyes that sting you like a handful of snow sliding down the back of your neck?"

"Not at all."

"The eyes that are lit with a flame you do not want to recognize?"

"It's nothing like that."

"The way his eyes dart back and forth, looking at every point around you but at no point where you are, even as he bears down on you?"

"No! A thousand times no!"

". . ."

"It's the way he looks at me afterwards, in the light, with a great sadness . . . like a father."

THE ROOM INSIDE MY FATHER'S ROOM

When I grew too big for my room, I forced the door open. My father was waiting for me in his favorite chair.

"I guess you're a man now," my father said. "Technically."

I looked around my father's room. It was at least three times as large as my room and wrapped itself around mine on two sides in the shape of an L.

"I've always hated that room," I said.

My muscles ached, and I tried to stretch out the kinks.

"I built that room for you, just like my father built this room for me." My father held out his palms, showing me his callouses.

"I notice your father made your room much bigger than you made mine!"

"I still needed space for me," my father said. He seemed embarrassed and wouldn't look me in the eye. "I was a grown man, and you were a child. Remember?"

Seeing him lounging in his chair made me angry. "I don't even have a place to sit in there!"

My father's lips curled up with his mustache. He got out of his chair and pointed a finger at my chest. "You know how ungrateful you are?" He spat on the floorboards. "Before you came along, my room was much larger! I even had a bed back then." He was towering over me, growing with indignation. But I was out of my room now and would not back down.

"I never asked to be born in that room," I said. I glared at him with a son's hate, and he seemed to shrink back down to my size, then smaller. Soon he collapsed into his chair.

"I did the best I could," he said to himself, barely above a whisper. "No one can say differently."

"Your best was shit," I said without much force. He was already weeping into his plate of sausages.

I couldn't stand to see him like that, but I also couldn't stand to go back into my tiny room inside my father's room. There were only two doors in his room. I opened the other and stepped into a room even larger than my father's. It was in the same shape, my father's room filling the upper right fourth.

This room was much messier though. The floor and walls were covered with old knickknacks and trinkets. Everything was coated in a film of dust.

My grandfather lay in his cot in the corner. "What do you want?" he said when he saw me. "Did your father send you to complain to me about how small his room is?"

"No, I'm looking for a bigger room for myself. I can barely fit in mine, plus the heat's broken."

"Well you can't stay here," my grandfather said. "There's barely enough space for me."

I was raised to respect my elders, but this made my blood bubble. His room was at least four times as large as my father's! I wanted to wrap my hands around his wrinkled throat. When I stepped forward, something crunched under my feet.

"This place is a mansion," I said. "It only looks small because you've filled it with old junk." I picked up the cracked baseball trophy and shook it for emphasis.

"Put that down," my grandfather screamed. "That's my thing. One of the only things I have left!" He pulled his old quilt up to his neck as if to shield himself from me.

"Look, I'll just sleep in the corner," I offered, "between those stacks of old magazines."

"Impossible!" he said, then he waved a finger in the air. "And if you think this is large, you should have seen *my* father's room. They built real solid rooms back in those days."

I sighed. "Well, maybe he's got a space for me then."

My grandfather merely laughed in response. He seemed lost in his old memories. He looked away from me and closed his eyes. As I left, I heard him beginning to snore.

My great-grandfather's room smelled thickly of mustard. His plates weren't cleared, and he was curled up on a massive canopy bed.

When I spoke, he looked up without recognition. Then he waved me toward his left ear.

My great-grandfather seemed sympathetic as he listened to my tale. I told him about my tiny room and the way his son and grandson had treated me. But when I was done, he shook his head.

"You can't stay here. Everyone gets their own room just for them."

"You don't understand how small my room is. It isn't fit for a man."

"Ha! I remember saying the same thing to *my* father when I was your age."

He reached up and tickled the hair behind my ears.

"Great-grandfather," I said in a tender voice I thought might appeal to his generation. "How about the other door? Can I find a room for myself through there?"

My great-grandfather slowly pointed at the door I had walked in from, which was still open.

"That door goes to the room I built for my son." He twisted

his body in the other direction. "And that door leads to my father's room."

"Does your father's room have an exit?"

"As far as I can remember, it's laid out the same way as mine. This is, mathematically, the most efficient way. I would advise you to lay out your own son's room in the same way, when that time comes." He smiled at me and shook his head knowingly. "Every young'un thinks they're a rebel. But we can only build what we know, and from the space we have."

I was so angry my nostrils were flaring. Then my anger turned to pity. My great-grandfather was even more small-minded than my grandfather and father! The whole lot of them were rotting away in their narrow rooms, never thinking of anything larger.

It was my turn to shake my head as I left his room.

Still, despite my distaste at that time, what my great-grandfather had said stuck with me, and many years later I repeated his words to my own son when he tried to start trouble.

The children erect a gallows out of desks, cardboard, and ribbon. A child is hung and then buried in the locker room under a pile of backpacks. The child is made to remain there, held down by two of the larger boys if necessary, for at least thirty seconds.

"Act properly!" I say.

They laugh, normally.

The children do not understand anything about death. When the time is up, the hanged classmate leaps from the locker room with a candy bar in his mouth. The other children cheer and clap.

Don't they realize that nothing returns from the dirt? Not ever? Death might as well be a lollipop to them.

Today's lesson is on sections of the house. I draw on the board with differently colored chalk.

"This is the hallway," I say. "This is the attic."

"My grandmother lives in the attic," says Norm.

"You lie!" says Sophie. "You don't have a grandmother."

"I do, I do! She lives in the attic in the sky."

Norm yanks her hair, and Sophie kicks his shin. They go on like this until I shout that there is no attic in the sky.

Carlos asks me where Norm's grandmother lives.

"The dirt," I say, pressing my hands to my face.

"Ew," Sophie says. "There are bugs down there."

I start telling them about my husband. The way they soaked his body with chemicals and then lowered him into the ground. But the children hold their hands to their throats and make gagging noises.

The next day, Carlos comes to school with one of his shoelaces tied around his neck. He is one of the most popular boys, and by naptime the entire class is wearing shoelace nooses.

They trip around the jungle gym at recess. I retrieve their laceless shoes from the yard and toss them in the cubbies.

After lunch, Sophie asks me if she can eat a chocolate bar. I tell her I only hand them out after pop quizzes.

"But I need chocolate to live!" she screams. Sophie starts shaking, rolling her eyes back until I can see only white.

"That is not funny!" I shout. "Not funny at all."

She is already beginning to giggle.

I get to class late on Friday. My eyes are red and sore from the night before.

When I walk into the room, the students are constructing a new gallows out of real wood and rope.

"It's for the science fair," Carlos says.

"What does this have to do with science?" I say.

"I dunno," says Norm.

"You're the teacher," says Sophie. "You tell us."

It doesn't seem to matter anymore. I sit at my desk and sip my burnt coffee.

When Sophie volunteers for a test run, I lift her body carefully to the loop. I'm supposed to hold her there while she pretends to die, then lower her safely to the ground.

The children count down their thirty seconds, but I keep

holding. I want them to get a little taste of fear. To realize death doesn't stop when you want it to.

Instead they just laugh as Sophie wiggles her body. The children fall to the floor and kick their legs in the air. Norm tumbles around on the ground like a hyena until he sweeps my legs out from under me.

I'm lying on the carpet, looking up at Sophie. Her face is as blue as a naptime mat.

The other children are standing or sitting around me. Some of them are beginning to cry. Carlos tugs on my skirt. It is almost recess.

Sophie's body is ticking back and forth, marking the seconds, minutes, hours left to fill before the day is done.

OUR NEW NEIGHBORHOOD

When the incidents start, my husband decides that what our neighborhood needs is a neighborhood watch. "We need to watch our assets as closely as we're going to watch the twins," he says, tapping the baby monitor screen. The screen is dark and blue. It shows two pale teddy bears in an otherwise empty crib.

The next morning, I come downstairs and see Donald slinking in the corner with a black trench coat and fedora. "What do you think?" he asks. We're low on disposable income, and, as usual, he bought a size too large.

"It looks a little conspicuous," I say.

"That's the idea, Margot. I want them to know someone is watching."

My husband buttons the top button of the coat, puts on a pair of sunglasses, and leaves. As I slide the toast into the toaster, I see him out the window. He's sneaking through the bushes in the neighbor's backyard.

The reason we're low on cash is that we poured our savings into buying House 32 in a neighborhood called Middle Pond. Middle Pond is located between West Pond on the west and East Pond on the east. All three are part of North Lake, which is itself a subset of the Ocean Shore suburb.

It looks perfect on paper. It has a stellar school system and all the amenities.

"Normally, I'd say we should wait and see," the real estate agent had said, "but if you don't snatch this now, you'll watch it go bye-bye."

Donald downloaded an app called HausFlippr that estimates property values in exclusive neighborhoods. Each time the Middle Pond score went up a full point, Donald cooked rib eyes on our new five-burner grill.

He hasn't cooked rib eyes in months.

Our neighbors aren't as worried about the declining rating. "My father used to say, 'markets fluctuate like fishes swim,'" John Jameson says at the neighborhood improvement meeting. It's our week to host, and I'm placing triangles of cheese beside rectangle crackers. Several of the other wives are insisting on helping me.

"We'll make sure this is the last time you host until after the miracles pop out," Janice Jameson says.

"Can I see?" Alice Johansson asks while lifting up the hem of my blouse.

"There's nothing to see. I'm not even showing."

In the other room, Donald is raising his voice. "Well *my* father always said you can never be too careful when it comes to property and prosperity. Plus, I already bought the trench coat."

The three of us walk back in holding the one tray.

"If it will make you feel better, we'll take a vote."

Donald is a tall, muscular man. He knows how to use his body, how to loom. The vote is tight, but Donald stares down enough neighbors to get his budget approved.

"Let's move on to the question of acceptable dye colors for next month's Easter egg hunt."

"I refuse to participate if metallics are allowed again," Claudia Stetson says. "They hurt my eyes."

. . .

The double-wide crib is temporarily in my office. This means that the baby monitor camera is temporarily in there too. It's shaped like a purple flower and situated between the plants on the windowsill. The monitor is downstairs in the living room. I've adjusted the angle of the camera so that it can see the crib but not my computer screen.

I can never allow Donald to see what I look at online.

The property values in Middle Pond are based on the reputation of the neighborhood, which is determined, in large part, by the official score assigned by the North Lake Committee on Proper Property Standards.

We are never told the qualifying factors. From the way the inspectors inspect, the list is long and varied. They inspect the level of seed in the bird feeders, observe the height of the grass in each lawn, and mark down rule infractions during games of sidewalk hopscotch.

Our neighbors probably thought Donald would get bored after a week or give up when the score increased. But the score keeps declining, and by midmonth Donald has an entire operation set up in our basement.

"Look at those paint stains in the Johanssons' driveway. And see how the Stetsons keep every curtain drawn?"

I'm maneuvering the laundry basket between his monitors and stacks of notes. He calls me over, makes me watch a time-lapse progression of black cars entering and leaving the Jacobsons' garage. "I'm going to see if the neighborhood board will increase the watch's budget. I need at least a dozen cameras. What do you think?"

I want to tell him my bladder hurts, my back aches, and I don't care about the neighbors' driveways. I want to tell him he was supposed to be helping me during the pregnancy, not getting in my way. Mostly, I want to tell him he should be looking at me, not the neighbors.

Or that's what I know I'm supposed to feel. In fact, I don't mind that Donald isn't looking at me.

I know every marriage goes through these phases, where you look at the other person and can't remember what you ever saw in them. I know it will pass, and that the babies will give us something new to look at together. But they aren't born yet.

When Donald starts pinning evidence to his corkboard, I creep upstairs and open my SingleMingle account. I gaze at the pixelated men. Some are smiling, with salt and wind in their hair. Others are introspective, reading a novel in a leather wingback chair. When I click next, a new one materializes. I click next again and again and again. There is an endless number of these men. My favorites are the ones who don't have shirts on. Some even crop their heads off, leaving disembodied torsos moving across my screen.

Donald's operation starts out small and consists mostly of warning signs he posts around the neighborhood. These signs show a dark figure with glowing eyes and the words "You Are Seen."

Nevertheless, during the inspector's next visit, while he is measuring the dampness of the cul-de-sac gutter, somebody keys his car. The next day, HausFlippr changes our safety rating from A to A- and drops our overall score five points.

Donald's budget is quickly tripled.

He buys a dozen cameras from Discountsleuth.com and hides them around our property. One is slinked through the hose, looking out at the street. Two face our immediate neighbors' houses through holes in the fence that Donald drills with an old dentist drill. One is hooked to the weathervane at the top of the house, providing a rotating view of the neighborhood as the wind blows.

The cameras snake down into the basement, where they are monitored by Donald and his two interns, Chet and Chad.

I use a fake zip code on my SingleMingle account. My user information is a lie. My height is shrunk an inch, my status marked "seductively single," my eyes labeled hazel instead of green. I use photos that obscure my features, angles that make my nose look bigger or my hair a different shade of brown. If anyone who knew me saw my profile, they wouldn't recognize me. Still, I make sure to browse strangers in other neighborhoods like North Forest and South Beach.

A man with the username OceanShoreStud27 catches my eye. His profile doesn't have much information, but I want to know more. I plug his user photos into reverse image searches, find his other profiles on other sites. His name is Derek Carrington. He's thirty-seven, a Libra, works in finance, has a blog devoted to his fishing catches. I check out his most played songs on WalkmanFM and a list of every movie he's rated on Filmglutton.com.

What gets my heart truly racing is the satellite photo of his house. It's only a few miles away and has a back porch and a pool. I zoom in as far as I can, until the pool's blue hues are giant pixelated blocks. I imagine myself sitting by the pool with Derek, our twins splashing in the abstract art.

I come.

I organize the files on Derek, zip and encode them on a folder in my external hard drive.

Then I start searching again.

"Corrupt assholes!" Donald is pounding his fist into the refrigerator. He notices me in the doorway, gazes at my stomach.

"What are the three of you craving? Fried chicken? Tacos? I can get one of the interns to make a run."

I tell him Indian, and he sends Chet. He looks at me with that serious expression he gets when he's unsure if I can handle what he wants to say. It's my least favorite expression of his.

"A dog attacked Chad while he was attaching a new camera to the Yield to Children sign. We got a photo, but none of the neighbors will identify it."

"People are protective of their pets."

"The bastards are trying to stonewall me!" He hits his palm with his fist. "It's not just violations, Margot. It's vandalism. Crime. Drugs. Lord knows what else."

He mistakes my confusion for worry. He comes over and touches my stomach with the backs of his hands. "Don't worry, I won't let anything happen to any of us." He continues to rub my belly with his knuckles. I try to think of the last time those knuckles touched me in a place I wanted to be touched.

"I wish I could see what's going on in there," he says without looking up.

Despite Donald's efforts, the incidents don't stop. Someone toilet papers the Thompsons' oak tree. A raccoon spills garbage across our cul-de-sac. Four yards have grown well beyond the allowable length. Donald calls in a half-dozen noise violations but can't pin down the sources.

He has successes too. He catches the Jamesons' cat urinating on the Abelsons' rosebushes, gets little Sally Henderson to sign an affidavit that she left her Frisbee in the gutter.

When we bought this place, Middle Pond houses were valued higher than West Pond and nearly equal with East Pond. Now they're no better than condos in South Creek.

Donald takes a temporary leave from his job. Says he's going to focus on the family, on our protection.

The North Lake Proper Property Standards Guidebook is a tome. Donald and his interns keep finding new rules and violations. Worse, he thinks the neighbors are undermining his efforts. They keep ripping the cameras out of the street lamps and snapping the microphones on the fire hydrants.

"It's probably just teens being teens," I say over dinner. This is the only time we see each other anymore. I spend all my time upstairs in the bedroom, adding men to my folder, while Donald spends it in the basement, monitoring his wall of screens.

He doesn't look up from his bowl of noodles. "Youth is no excuse for crime. If you don't stop them now, they'll be watching the world from behind bars."

The nurse squirts the gel, fires up the machine.

I'm not sure what to think of the little objects on the screen. Intellectually, I know they're our children. But they look like microbes in a microscope, inscrutable creatures from another world.

"Those are the hearts. Those are the brains," the nurse is saying. She uses a little laser pointer on the screen.

"The checkup comes with prints, right?" Donald asks. "I want to be able to look at these whenever I need to."

As my belly swells, my searching habits shift. I've gotten bored gathering information on strangers in distant neighborhoods, started to yawn seeing the photos of middle-aged men next to their cars and fireplaces. I move on from SingleMingle to other, more explicit, sites. Affluent Affairs, OkDungeon, WASPsGoneWild.

I set my zip code to Middle Pond, check in on the neighbors. Browsing close to home, I have to obscure myself further. I use photo-editing software to change the tint of my skin. I make sure there are no identifiable objects in the background of my selfies, or else gussy up my wall with dime-store decorations that I throw away after a snap. I get the latest encryption software to mask my IP.

The men on these sites are like me. They don't reveal their faces, don't give away identifying information. I stare at a hand or corner of a painting caught in the background of a photo and try to figure out who I'm looking at. Are those William Carlson's pale thighs? Do those pubes curl how I'd imagine James Jacobson's curl? Is that edge of cheek or lock of hair one I've seen at a neighborhood meeting?

The North Lake Committee on Proper Property Standards applauds Donald, gives him an award for excellence in property protection. He makes me come to the ceremony. It's the first time we've been out together in weeks. These days, the twins move so much I'm peeing every thirty minutes. For the most part I stay upstairs, logged in.

As usual, Donald's speech is overlong and mawkish, yet sprinkled with sharp wit. I'm too far along to drink but I try to will myself drunk by staring intensely at the glasses of merlot. I pee twice during the speech.

The residents of Middle Pond, however, are not happy with the neighborhood watch. "You scared Sally," Hubert Henderson says when the Hendersons come by for dinner two nights later.

"She wouldn't be scared if she didn't have something to hide." Donald chews his pork chop slowly, eyes rotating back and forth between the Hendersons.

"Look, this has gone on long enough. This neighborhood doesn't need a watch. If anything, you're making people uncomfortable and they're acting out!"

Donald gets up, wipes his chin with a napkin. He goes into the other room.

"Why, I never," Henrietta says. She turns to me. "You understand our concern, right? You have children on the way. This isn't the inner city. You don't want them spied on all the time, do you?"

I'm not really paying attention to her. I'm looking at the curve of Hubert's elbow, mentally measuring the distance between moles on his neck. Have I seen those body parts before?

Donald comes back and slaps down a manila folder. It's stuffed with papers and has "Hendersons" written on the front in Magic Marker letters.

"What is the meaning of this?" Hubert says.

When he opens it, the folder is filled with photos of him and his family. Secret shots of Sally failing to wipe her muddy shoes on the welcome mat, close-ups of fungal infections on the front-yard trees, stills of the cat devouring a protected songbird. He flips through them with increasing speed.

"This is madness!" Hubert sputters.

"It's a reckoning," Donald says.

The neighborhood association cuts off the watch's funding, but Donald doesn't care. "It just means we're on to something."

He shows me grainy footage of neighbors wearing black stockings on their heads and ripping out his cameras. He freezes them, puts them side by side with photos taken from their FaceFriends pages. I lean forward, inspecting these same photos from my files on a new screen.

The next week, Donald takes out a home equity loan. He puts the money into three iSpy drones. They can fly up and down the neighborhood for two hours before they need to be recharged. Each has a camera on a swivel base. "These babies are the future of neighborhood protection," he says.

I watch the test run from my upstairs window. Chet and Chad set up chairs on the front lawn. They cheer each time the drones pass by.

Middle Pond feels like a ghost town. Children are no longer allowed to play games in the streets. No one walks their dogs or barbeques on their lawn. Our neighbors don't want to have every action watched, every interaction documented. They stay inside with the curtains drawn. Most of them have purchased tinted windows for their cars so Donald can't see how many come and go.

The only things that move on the streets are the drones, humming in their preprogrammed patterns.

I can barely even move indoors. My belly is swollen, and when I look at myself in the mirror, I don't recognize myself. I know it won't be long before the twins are born, and that their birth will mean a change to much more than just my body or our house.

I've installed the Bread Crumb app on Donald's phone. The app shows you a digital trail to your device's location, so that you can find if it's misplaced. I use it to monitor Donald's movements, see where he is coming from or going to.

"Donald, maybe you can drive us to the movies. Have a night out for ourselves before the house is full of screams."

"Can't now, Margot. Things are coming together. I'm connecting the threads. This thing goes all the way to the top." He is breathing heavily on the phone. We never see each other in the flesh anymore. The house is divided between our bases of operation. When I call him for something, Donald sends one of the interns upstairs.

"The top of what, Donald?"

"You don't want to know."

●●●

I wait for the drone to fly past, then close the blinds. Today I'm finishing my file on John Jameson. I found him on SuburbanPervs, recognized his sprinkler system in the background of an explicit pic.

It only takes a few clicks to get his credit score, high school GPA, and family tree. I put the details in my spreadsheet, gaze at the figures. You can look at all that data, and the picture of a person emerges. It really does. I know more about Jameson now that most of his friends, more perhaps than even his wife.

Suddenly, I get a pop-up chat from Jameson's profile, Silver_Fox_Golfer. "I think you've been looking at me," he says.

I don't reply.

"I've had my eye on you too," he says. He puts in a request for a video chat. "If you record, I'll sue."

Outside, things are getting ugly. The neighborhood watch is opposed by a new group, the Middle Pond Citizens' Veil. The MPCV scuffle in the streets with Chad and Chet. They cover all the watch signs with their own symbol, a child skipping rope with a hood over her head.

The exact membership of the MPCV is unknown. They wear latex masks that have been fashioned to look like Donald. I do a double take when I see a group of Donalds on the sidewalk in front of our house, erecting a temporary wall.

Donald responds by attaching speakers to the drones and blasting out audio clips of the neighbors admitting their violations and begging for forgiveness, which were recorded during clandestine interrogation sessions with Chet and Chad in our basement.

Donald is secretly receiving funds from the North Lake Committee, whose management is concerned the destabilization of property standards will spread beyond Middle Pond. I know this because I've started monitoring Donald's e-mails—his password is ShirleyandHugh2016, his desired names for our twins and the year of their upcoming birth.

"Donald, you're our man on the inside," the most recent encrypted e-mail says. "Remember the three c's of neighborhood standards: Community, Commitment, and Containment. Emphasis on containment. This can't be allowed to spread."

While I'm trying to use public information to answer Frederick Abelson's uCloudPhotos security questions, a brick smashes though the window. The double-wide crib is covered in shards of glass. I wobble to the window and see a Donald-faced figure climbing over our fence.

There is a sheet of paper attached to the brick. It says, "Do you want out? Check [ ] Yes [ ] No. Sincerely, the MPCV."

I think about this question for some time. Out of what? The neighborhood? My marriage? My soon-to-be-formed family? My life?

If I could go back and do things differently, well, of course I would. But isn't that true of everyone?

I mark my check. Then I place the letter in a paper shredder.

The twins anchor me to my desk chair. I can no longer see my toes when I stand up, and the hormones and chemicals swirling inside me are making my body feel like an alien vessel.

The main thing it feels is hunger. Chet and Chad bring me take-out meals, but Donald remains a ghost floating in the glow of his basement monitors. I see him only through a small camera that I tucked behind the washing machine. When I installed it, I saw something that broke my heart just a little bit. Above his workstation there were two images: a map of the neighborhood and the sonogram printout. There were pins and string connecting the image of the twins to the map of our neighborhood, permanent marker notations on the side. I couldn't make out the chicken scrawl code.

A part of me thinks that when all of this is over, it might not be impossible for us to go back to the life we had. We could delete all the data we've accumulated, purge the audio and video. Live again like our neighbors are strangers that we simply wave to on the street. Why not? Every day people reset their lives, move to new towns or take up new jobs.

But then an explosion echoes down the street.

The flaming car is not our car. Donald doesn't know what happened, and there is no clear footage as the drones were captured in nets strung between the street lamps on the cul-de-sac right before the attack.

The explosion pulls the different factions out into their yards: the neighborhood watch on ours, the MPCV and its sympathizers on the others. The air is thick with tension and smoke.

"This is a declaration of war," Chet says.

"Each house is either with us or against us," says Chad.

"You two don't even live in this neighborhood," I say.

Chet scratches his ear. "Well, we get college credit if the mission here succeeds."

Donald pulls me close, moves his body in front of me as if to shield me from the neighbors' eyes. "I'll find out who did this," he whispers to me. "I have cameras they don't even know about, feeds beyond their wildest dreams."

The driver is singed and shouting, "No, no, no! What the fuck?" No one moves to help him. His clothes are still slightly on fire. He looks around at all of us. He's wearing a pointed purple hat with embroidered stars. His pointer finger is outstretched, and he moves it from family to family, yard to yard. "What kind of neighborhood is this?" he shouts. He says that this was only his first week driving the Wizsearch street-mapping car. Wizsearch has been expanding into online maps and is trying to get real-life pictures of every street. "It's supposed to be a public service. If you didn't want to be mapped, you could have opted out online!"

"You look just about ready to burst," Diane Abelson says. She's standing in my doorway holding a casserole dish. She lets out a forced, high-pitched laugh.

"Another month or so to go," I say. I'm thankful my belly is large enough to obscure my laptop screen. I reach my hand behind my back to close it.

Diane's eyes dart around the room. She mouths something that I can't make out. "I brought you my famous third-trimester tortellini!" Now she's talking much more loudly than necessary. "I ate this for a month straight with both Bobby and Susan!"

She hands me the casserole dish and then slides a note into my pocket. She steps back into the hallway and scans to see if anyone is there. "Well, I better be going. Hope to *hear* from you soon."

After she leaves, I read the note. It tells me they know the room is bugged, so they can't talk. They want to know if I can broker a peace meeting, get the two sides to come to terms. "There is a phone in a plastic bag in the middle of the casserole. Use it outside, and Donald won't be able to monitor it. Call us if you can help end the madness."

I drag all of my files—every neighbor I've gathered data on, each .doc of their life and .xls of their history—and place them in the recycle bin. I tell myself it's unhealthy to spend so much time monitoring the lives of others and so little time looking at my own. Plus, when the twins finally arrive, I won't have time to look up my neighbors and video chat with masked faces. I'll be shaking brightly colored toys before their newborn eyes or watching to make sure they don't eat rat poison or loose nails.

I hover my cursor over the trash can icon. I click on it, and my breath gets short. I hit undo, sending the files flying back to the proper folders. There will always be time to delete them after the twins are born. I'll be able to make a clean break when that happens.

Until then, I fire up the browser and log back in.

And then one morning I wake up and the neighborhood is quiet. I don't hear the drones flying past. I don't hear Chet and Chad struggling with masked Donalds. I don't even hear the sounds of cars driving quickly down the street.

I get up and pee, wash my hands with antibacterial soap. I struggle to the window.

At the end of the street, I see two people being shoved into a patrol car. The rest of the houses have their driveways blocked off with police tape.

I move to my laptop, do a Wizsearch News search for "Middle Pond." No results.

I look over at the casserole phone still in its plastic bag. I dial the preprogrammed contact, listen to it go straight to voicemail.

Someone taps spryly on the door.

Donald extends a handful of roses. His face is shaved, and he's wearing a new suit that fits just right. He looks nothing like the disheveled figure hunched over his charts in the basement I've been monitoring.

"It's all over, baby. We won, you and me."

My heart is beating quickly, and I'm unsure what combination of fear, relief, and confusion is mixing in my head.

He hugs me and tells me he's taken down the cameras and will be renting the drones out for overhead photos of upscale weddings. "The North Lake Committee asked me to give you this." He hands me a pendant of an eye surrounded by a white picket fence. The bottom says, "Sponsored by Wizsearch."

"There will be a ceremony later, of course." He pins it carefully to my blouse. "Margot, I have to say I had my doubts about you for a little while. I thought you were looking for kicks elsewhere, but I couldn't see the big picture. Obviously you knew I was monitoring your online activities. You knew I'd copy your files. Your research was the key to the whole operation's success. The data you had on the neighbors exposed it all: tax fraud, drug use, and everything else we needed to take them down."

Donald takes me by the hand and leads me downstairs and out onto our front porch. "There'll be a housing depression for a little while, but with the bad elements gone, the market will stabilize before the twins are even in preschool."

We step onto the trimmed green grass. I can feel the twins swimming inside me. The empty neighborhood they will be born into surrounds us. I look at the facade of the house across the street. It is similar to our house, but different. It has the garage on the left, and ours has the garage on the right.

NORTH AMERICAN MAMMALS

FILLING POOLS

People say I have a baby face. You can look at me and pretend I'm drowning. I do this watery thing with my eyes. How you work the face is important in this line of work. Window to the soul and all that.

"Your child's childhood ain't your momma's childhood," I tell the woman at the door. "Don't let nostalgia get in the way of safety."

She has a six-year-old wrapped around her leg and a baby hooked into her arm. I can tell this lady is one who craves the visuals.

"One moment you're sipping ice tea on your lawn chair," I say, rubbing my boot across the welcome mat. "The next moment, your little girl has bonked open her head on the bottom, chlorine rinsing her brain."

The mom gets a twitch in her eye when I say that.

I fill in the deep ends of pools door-to-door. Make them all an even shallow. Learned how from videos online. It's a better business than you might think. All I have is a sump pump, a cement mixer, and some cans of blue paint. I had some other things, like a backhoe and a minivan, before the divorce. Now Sarah, my ex, has those things. Well, not the backhoe. The city repossessed that and then gave me a nice big fine.

. . .

The cement truck is mine and custom-made. A commercial cement mixer hooked up to the back of an '82 Ford.

"Is that thing up to regulation?" the woman at the door asks.

"Fuck the regulations," I tell her. "We're talking about children's lives."

I study faces a lot. I used to be a painter. I even sold a few portraits to Sarah's family, before the divorce. The woman in the doorway has a trustworthy face, soft and fuzzy like a TV interview lady.

"Is the mister around?" I say.

"I'm afraid the mister isn't ever around," the lady says, looking down at the little girl. "He is, uh, on a long vacation."

I nod my head sympathetically, offer a discounted rate, and hand over my card.

It all started when this showboat was doing backflips at night in the community pool. Apparently he had the deep end mixed up with the shallow. His lady friend ran screaming down the street buck naked.

I was there when they fished him out. If you wanted to see a good face, you should've seen his. All pop-eyed and head flopping around like a fish. It was disquieting.

The community was in an uproar on account of both this and the toddler who'd drowned last year during swim class, but City Hall wasn't doing anything. I knew a business opportunity when I saw one. Sarah was walking out the door for girls' night and gave me a face like, *Boy, I hope you know what you're doing.*

My first job, so it was kinda lumpy. But there were a few people who might have said I was a hero. One newspaper did, and I carry a clipping around to show the customers.

· · ·

I think my favorite faces are the faces of children. Like the next day, when I'm back at the lady's house, lowering a sump pump into the deep, and the little six-year-old is smushing her pudgy face right into the chain-link fence.

"What's your name?"

"Petunia," she says.

"Oh," I say, "like the flower."

"No!" she shouts.

I hook up the hose to the pump and turn that sucker on. The girl's face gets all white and she runs inside.

It's a hot day, and I sit on a deck chair under a faded blue umbrella. Watching all that water being sucked into the sewer makes me wish I had a beer. A few minutes later, Petunia is back outside stuffing fish sticks in her face. She hands me one through the fence. It's still a bit frozen on the inside, but I swallow anyway.

"Thanks," I say. I can see her mother watching behind the glass door. I give a little wave, flash my kindly neighbor face.

"Come around if you want," I say, and I lie down in one of the pool chairs, listen to the sump pump churn. The sound reminds me that I need to call my ex-wife.

Straight to voicemail.

"It's good to hear your voice, Sarah," I say. "Wondering if you can give me Bob's number." Bob's our old plumber. I've got a burst seal in my basement. I pump it out every morning, but there's a new pool each night. "Let's let bygones be bygones. Also, let me know if you want to get coffee sometime."

While I'm on the phone, Petunia opens the gate and sits down on a fun noodle near the pool's edge. I click the phone off, stuff it in my pocket.

"Why are you filling in our pool?" she says with an angry face.

"Just the deep end, baby-doll."

"Why are you filling in the deep end?"

"So you don't die."

She frowns and eats another fish stick. She walks to the edge and kicks a floaty duck into the pool, watches it lower inch by inch.

Backyard deep ends can go up to ten feet deep, which I level out to four. That's a lot of cement. Sometimes I toss little things down as it dries. A plastic truck or some coins, makeup or jewelry Sarah left at the house, whatever is around. They get covered up and left where no one will ever find them. You could fold a few bodies into that goop before it hardens.

After a day's work, I like to just drive around looking for splashes of blue over the fences. I keep a map of potential clients. What's funny about these neighborhoods is you drive around them enough, and they start to feel like a giant maze. You can't remember where anything is supposed to be. The faces of each house look the same as the last.

I give Sarah another call and again she doesn't pick up.

"How much of this is a man supposed to take, Sarah?" I say. "This is my fucking basement we're talking about! It's growing a weird mold."

I pull into my driveway, go inside, and flip on the TV.

I'm back the next day, mixing up the cement. Petunia is squatting on the noodle, singing a song. The mother gives us mugs of lemonade.

I'm watching the gray bits swirl together and thinking about Sarah, the way she thinks she can treat me, when Petunia pulls on my wallet chain.

"Why are you sad?" she says.

"What?" I say.

I make my face look confused for a while. Then the mother comes sprinting up with the cordless still in her hand. She's holding the baby tight in the other.

"I've got an emergency," the lady says to me.

I give her a nonchalant wave, tell her I'll be okay. She puts her arm around Petunia, smothers her against her knees.

It's her father, she mouths. *She can't see him.*

"Can you keep an eye on Petunia?" she says out loud.

"Sure," I say, "protecting children is my job." I give her the all-business smile and Petunia the silly-clown smile. Petunia winces. Her mother pulls her inside and gives me a string of thank-yous and curses.

The cement takes quite some time to dry after you've flattened it out, so I go inside to wash the gunk off my hands, maybe find the little girl a bag of fruit snacks or a stack of crackers.

The house isn't that large, but it feels comfortable and calm. The walls are decorated with framed family photos and paintings of running dogs. It feels like the place Sarah and I always thought we'd have, although Sarah was a calico cat girl. I didn't like having to clean up after her's but liked the look of its furry tortoiseshell face. When she left, she took the cat too.

Petunia is at a computer playing with cartoon hippos.

"Is that educational?" I ruffle her hair a little, give her a pinch on the cheek.

"Can I have a juice box?" she says.

"Sure thing, sweet pea."

It feels good helping out a family in need. I walk to the fridge and fish out a grape juice for Petunia, then search around until I find some whiskey. I pour a little into my mug with a picture of a beaver and the phrase "too much dam work to do" and walk around the house checking out the different rooms.

Something about the blue mug, with its comical phrase printed on the front, makes me feel like a father as I stroll through the rooms. Like this could have been the castle I was king of if things had happened a little differently. And who knows, maybe I could have something like this someday still.

I try Sarah yet again. "Hi, Sarah," I say. "You'd never believe where I am right now!"

I'd thought it was the voicemail again, but it was her actual voice.

"What the fuck do you think you're doing, Burt?" she screams. "I don't have any goddamn number of any goddamn plumber. Call me one more time though, and I'll use the number of the goddamn police!"

"Now hold on," I say, but she's already hung up.

I walk back to the kitchen, pour some more whiskey. I go to the couch and sit and stew. Then, I don't know why, but I just start to cry.

Petunia comes over, and I cover my eyes, pretend I'm laughing at something on TV.

"I knew you were sad," she says. She puts her little hand on my shoulder.

"It's nothing."

"Tell me about it," she says. She gives me a serious look, like a cartoon psychologist.

"It's just my ex," I say. "She twisted my heart like a bendy straw."

"My mommy always says you have to stand up for yourself," she says. "That's the only way people will respect you."

I take another gulp of whiskey, shrug my shoulders. She keeps asking me questions, and all I can say is that I don't know how things ended up like this. I don't know anything. I get a refill of whiskey and offer Petunia another juice box.

"You need to tell her how you feel, right now!" she says suddenly.

"We should wait here while the cement dries," I say, waving my hand toward the window.

"No!" Petunia shouts. "Right now, mister." She gives me this face that makes me think, *Out of the mouths of babes*, you know?

I scribble a note for the mother on the door with the relevant details.

"Road trip!" Petunia says, her little hands filled with plastic-wrapped snacks.

I check on the cement. I'd forgotten to take out the floaty duck, and its yellow butt is popping right out of the gunk.

We peel out of the driveway in my truck. I turn on a little rock 'n' roll on the radio.

"This okay? I don't know what the Barney station is."

Petunia is opening a pack of Oreos. I can feel the whiskey working in me, and I roll down the windows, let the summer air in. I take a left at the light and then a right after the children-crossing sign.

"How much farther?" Petunia says.

"Not much," I say, but after we've been driving a while, I realize I can't remember the way. I know Sarah now lives on a road named after a kind of tree. Is it Sycamore or Sugar Maple?

We keep driving through the flat suburban grid. I try to sneak a look over the fences for possible clients.

"I'm tired," Petunia says.

"Did we already pass that house?" I ask. I stick my head out the window, try to remember if I've seen those garden gnomes already. The phone starts ringing in the loose change pit of my car.

"Sarah. Speak of the devil."

"Sarah? This is Cynthia Hartman," a female voice says. "Is this Burt the cement man?"

"The very same."

The voice gets louder. "Where the hell are you? And where is my daughter?"

"Don't worry, we'll be back in a jiffy," I say. "We're just finishing a little errand. Can't talk now."

I turn the wheel this way and that. We drive past dogs and children running around well-trimmed yards. Some of them try to wave at us as we pass.

"I want to go back," Petunia says. All her snack wrappers are empty and shining on her lap.

"Come on, Petunia," I say. "It's right around the corner, I'm sure of it."

We turn on Spruce Street, take a left onto Sapling. I'm drumming on the steering wheel in anticipation. We can't go back now. I've got things I need to say to Sarah, things that need to be said right now.

"I want Mommy. I want to go home," she says.

The phone keeps jiggling around in the dish.

"It has got to be right around here," I say.

I turn onto Sequoia Street. Petunia's face is getting red and starting to crinkle.

"It's gonna be great, Petunia," I say. "Don't you worry. The two of us will let Sarah know what's what," I say. "You and I will show her she needs to reconsider things. And if she doesn't answer the door, we'll use the mixer and pour it right onto the doorstep. Cement her right in!" I give a little laugh. "Can you imagine? I can't wait to see the look on her face!"

HIKE

Cheryl huffed off, which she could do because Paul had a gimpy knee. They were strolling through the yellowed leaves of fall. Cheryl thought sometimes the only way to talk to Paul was to march away in silence.

The trail went all over the place, moving up and down the hills, turning back on itself.

Cheryl came across an overweight man lying in the middle of the path. His son was sitting on a log, playing a game on his cell phone.

"Just go around me," the man said, panting. Were these the same people Cheryl raced against to get to the shortest line at the grocery store?

She looked the other way as she skirted past. Cheryl had grown up in this town, left, come back, left, and come back again so many times that even seeing the welcome sign made her dizzy.

God, she was thirsty! Why had she left the water bottle with Paul? There was a thin creek worming beside the path. She stopped to splash some water on her face.

Paul materialized around the bend.

"Cheryl!" he said, waving his hands. "You're going the wrong way. This is the Robin trail, we agreed on Blue Jay."

He always had to say something like that.

"Wait. I've got the granola."

Cheryl ran back to the signpost. This time she took the path with two blue lines painted on the oak tree. Small birds sat in the trees singing songs like bratty children. Cheryl looked straight ahead and tried to forget herself and blend into the woods.

There was something uncanny about the changing mood of the land. One second you were in an enchanted forest, the next you emerged on a ruinous pile of broken rocks. It was like walking through sets of different Hollywood films.

Paul would never understand the way you have to impose your will on the land.

Here is another thing Cheryl hated: the way Paul dug his knuckles into the dimple of her tailbone when he thrust from behind.

Cheryl passed an elderly couple holding hands. They didn't know which way to move, and she ended up ducking beneath and knocking their hands apart.

"Slow down!" the old lady shouted.

Instead, Cheryl descended into the shade of the valley. The trees looked like cancer patients in their yellowing leaves. Tumorous fungi lined the damp trunks.

The trail rounded a bend and split into two more trails. You can never really reach the end of anything!

Cheryl felt sad and tired. She hoped Paul was sadder and even more tired. Maybe they could tire each other out enough that they could shut up and go home and take a hot bath or watch a movie. She couldn't even remember what Paul had said, or what she thought he had said, or even what he had thought she had said that made him say it to begin with.

Someone was whimpering behind her. Cheryl turned and found a woman in a red windbreaker crouched in the leaves. When she looked at Cheryl, her face was pink and wet.

"I followed him here, and he did it again!"

"Who are you? And how do you know Paul?" Cheryl demanded.

"I'm not talking about Paul. I'm talking about Eric."

The woman led Cheryl a little way through the woods to a secret swimming hole. Cheryl stood on a boulder to get a better look. The pool's water was black in the shade. On a flat rock beside the water, she could see one pale body bouncing up and down on another.

"He said he loved me. Don't words mean anything anymore?" The woman wiped her tears on Cheryl's sweatshirt and tried to hug her. Down on the rock, the couple humped away.

Cheryl was not thinking of Paul when she picked up a stick and tossed it in a blind arc. It spun around down onto the man's clenched buttocks, causing him to yell and roll off the woman. He fell into the swimming hole with a quiet splash.

"Perverts!" the naked woman shouted, pointing at them. She was scrambling for her clothes. "The woods is full of perverts!"

Cheryl felt relief flow through her. She turned and smiled at the woman next to her, her new sister in a world of shitty men.

"Why did you do that?" the woman said. Her face scrunched up as she stepped backwards.

"I thought that's what you wanted," Cheryl said.

"You have to let me confront things on my own terms," she said.

The naked woman was running deeper into the woods, and the man was staring up at Cheryl.

"Hey!" the naked man said to Cheryl, clothes clutched to his crotch. "Aren't you in my yoga class? Charlotte, right? Or Charlene?"

Cheryl left them all there shouting and tried to find a path without people. She followed the curve of the valley and then ascended on the far hills. Bright lichens covered everything.

Before Paul there had been Theodore, and before Theodore there had been Christopher, Jeremy, Karl, Andy, and Abraham. And there was another horrible line of them waiting in the future, with even worse names like Kevin and Camden. She could feel all of them groping her with endless clammy palms.

That was not to let women off the hook, especially not mothers like Paul's, who would back her against the kitchen sink, stab a finger into one of Cheryl's ovaries, and ask, "When are you going to stop letting these go to waste?"

The sun broke through a fist of clouds. Cheryl was looking up at the treetops when she felt a stick smack against her shin. "Shit!" she yelled.

A small girl and her even smaller brother were standing in front of her. The boy was whirling a stick around and making zapping noises with his mouth. The girl was staring up at Cheryl with a broken stick in her hand and a pout on her face.

"You broke my wizard stick," the girl said.

"And you said the s word," the boy added. He whacked his sister's jacket and said, "Shazam!"

The girl didn't acknowledge her brother. She kept looking at Cheryl and made her eyes start to water.

"Okay, okay," Cheryl said. She walked into the woods and tried to rip a thin branch off a sycamore. It clung surprisingly to life. Eventually she just picked an appropriate-sized stick off the forest floor, which the girl grabbed without even a thank-you.

"You want to see a Death Fire Spell? I'll show you a Death Fire Spell!"

The two ran off down the path. Cheryl was feeling tired and leaned against a large tree with dark red leaves. Maybe Paul could be the end, she thought. She did love Paul during certain hours of certain days. How many hours did you have to love someone to be in love?

She felt something crawling on her neck. Ants poured out of the bark.

Cheryl ran up a pathless hill, swinging her arms around to ward off branches and small plants. She thought if she got to the top she would be able to spot Paul.

There was a plastic bag full of Chunky soup cans tied up at the overlook. The large rocks were piled up with deep cracks, and Cheryl wondered what kinds of beasts or snakes might leap out at her. She climbed to the top of the rocks and looked out across the valleys and toward the shrunken town. Autumn was spreading with crackling orange and red leaves, like the path of a teenage pyromaniac. There was even a little house ablaze on the side of the hill, smoke worming toward the clouds. Through breaks in the trees, she could see fire trucks the size of toys racing up the slope.

"My cans!"

"What now?" Cheryl said, turning. A man covered in dirt and bits of dead leaves was crawling out of a crevice. He crouched on the rocks and thrust his hand toward her. Where did they keep coming from?

The man was holding out a rusty blade. His face was one giant beard with eyes attached.

"What are you talking about?" she asked.

"My cans," he said, a little sadder now.

She looked over at the sack of canned goods hanging from the tree. The man was inching toward her across the massive rocks.

"I don't want your stupid cans or anything else," she said.

The man made small swipes with the knife.

She pulled the bag off the branch and swung it at the bearded man. It hit him in the knee, and he let out a loud growl before tumbling off the rock.

Cheryl looked down at where the man had fallen and saw

bits of blood on the rocks. The sun was beginning to go down, and his body was mostly in shadows. It was very quiet. The man's hands twitched their last twitches. A bird watched with a cocked head from the neighboring rock.

"Cheryl!" a voice said down the hill. Of all people, it had to be Paul.

Cheryl gazed down into the crevice where the man had come from. She could lower herself down there with ease, live a new life in these woods.

Paul was working his way up the hill. Cheryl stood there at the peak. It was another in an unending succession of situations in which she had no interest in learning what it was she was required to do.

THE DEER IN VIRGINIA

Or take the day my father handed me his glass of lemonade and reached for the rifle. My mother had gone inside to fetch a tray of crackers. My father's hands no longer worked well, and he asked me to pump the gun. I did so as silently as I could.

"Watch this," he said into the chamber as he held it against his shoulder with both hands.

It was his birthday, and the backyard was drunk on the green nonsense of spring. Below us, a group of deer nibbled on my mother's daffodils. Suddenly they became as stiff as cardboard cutouts. The rifle was only an air rifle, my present to him that day. It came with a sandwich bag of silver pellets. Deer were everywhere in Virginia. They had been my whole life. When I was a child, I would watch my father hurl baseballs at the deer in our yard as I ate my cereal. Now his pitching arm ached, and the only thing he wanted for his birthday was a BB gun.

I had returned to town because it was all I had left. Everything else I'd lost or had sneaked away in the night: my friends, my job, my apartment in the city, and you, my almost wife.

My father only wanted to drive the deer back into the woods, but when he fired, the pellet rode a gust of wind into the largest deer's eye. This sent it frantically sprinting into the trunk of an old oak tree. The body dropped into the mulch beside the tree trunk where, growing up, I had hidden cigarettes

and cheap beer. The others leapt away in different directions. The sunlight was peeking over the distant hills and into
our eyes.

Or else another time, when you and I were fighting on a four-
hour drive through West Virginia in the rain. We were back
together for what I thought would be the time that lasted, but
along the way things had collapsed again. You had a blue scarf
tied around your throat and the window down three inches to
let out your cigarette smoke. We were fighting over something
one of us had said. I was driving, and you were turning up a
country station, the only one that came in, as loud as you could
when a small buck darted out from the trees. I swerved to dodge
it and barely held on to the road. The car made its way in and
out of the gutter and continued straight as if nothing had happened. You turned the radio off, and we were silent for a while
before we both began to laugh. The storm was starting to peter
out. We emerged from the shade of highway trees into fields of
wheat and a bright sun that, for a brief second, made everything
look as if it was wrapped in cellophane.

Then ten miles later, we stopped at a gas station because the
car didn't seem to be accelerating correctly. We thought maybe
a tire had popped, but when we stepped out of the car, we saw
the trail of red and fur and, underneath, the buck with its head
twisted in the front axle, its wet body hiding behind the wheels
like a playful child.

So many days seem to end this way: bewildered, standing
in a town I do not know with a person who might as well be
a stranger, and the windshield wipers flicking specks of rain
against my cheek.

HALFWAY HOME TO SOMEWHERE ELSE

The baby had been bawling since the West Virginia border, so I figured we could use a break. We were driving by a series of hot dog joints in a town called King's Crossroad. I don't think any king had ever visited there, but the pilgrims that built this land had a zeal for history. I took a right turn by a shack selling flags and T-shirts, Confederate and tie-dye mostly. It was hippie hillbilly country.

"This not our exit," my wife said in her broken English, turning down the radio with her cigarette hand. The other was holding the baby to her open-air boob.

"I thought we could use a little break."

"Your trip," she said. She took a drag and blew it carefully out the open window and away from the baby's face.

It was one of those muggy days where the sun licked you all over like a stray dog. The kind of day that wore on you. All you wanted was some lemonade, but the little boys and girls were inside with the TV and AC, and the paper cups were being chewed apart by angry rats.

I did like driving with the windows down though.

"There's an old swimming hole around here I used to go to," I said. "We can cool ourselves down."

"My swimsuit in bottom of bag," my wife said. "And what the hell is swimming *hole?*"

A bearded trucker leaned out of his window as he drove

past. My wife flicked him off and tucked her breast back into her cutoff shirt.

"You can change at the hole," I said. "It's an old stone quarry. Some digging machine went too deep and hit an underground spring, and now you can swim there. We used to go all the time in school. The machine is still under there, near the south side. One time, a kid at the rival high school did a swan dive too far down and ripped open his belly on the rusted metal. It was in all the newspapers."

Clouds of gnats bounced off our windshield.

"That's horrible," my wife said. "That's another horrible thing you tell me."

Maybe here I should say that Natasha was my mail-order bride. At least that's what she liked to say. I brought her over to work at my restaurant, a waitress exchange program with one of those splintered-off Soviet countries I used to confuse. We served Southern food with an haute cuisine twist. Mango salsa rub on the fried chicken, wasabi-coated French fries, that kind of spineless bastardization. Natasha wasn't the best waitress, but she had fierce, sad eyes and whispered nasty jokes about the customers into my ear. Her fingers were pale, thin bones with limp ash perpetually growing between them. She didn't even seem to mind when I grunted my sorrows between her legs on the wiped-down bar after closing. She just smoked her black Russian cigarettes and scratched my neck, saying, "It is okay."

When her work visa expired, what were we supposed to do? Natasha didn't want to go back to her "rotten land filled with crooks and assholes," and I, while still young, was old enough to know the scarcity of steady sex, and anyway Natasha was now my floor manager, and business was booming.

I only got lost once looking for the old quarry. I took us

down an unmarked gravel road that kicked up so much dust we had to roll up the windows.

"You make me waste smoke," Natasha said.

At the end of the road we found an old farmhouse, maybe from the plantation days. The paint still looked white, but dried vines reached up the walls. The dust cloud collapsed on our windshield. I had to use three squirts to wipe it off. Looking around, we saw the yard was filled with scrap-iron unicorns. They were belly deep in crabgrass. There was at least a half dozen of these welded beasts: the sculptures of either a bored heiress or a schizophrenic squatter.

"This what I love about this country," Natasha said without elaboration. She took a snapshot out the window, and we backed away.

"Must be the other way," I said.

"Must," my wife said.

The baby said nothing but reached out to me as a dribble of spit spilled down her puckered lips. I stuck a finger in her hand, and she squeezed it and laughed as I drove.

Natasha and I had gotten in another ten months before an Asian Tex-Mex fusion joint opened up across the street, and my customers scampered away. Their tempura tacos had been rated best in the South by *Gourmet*. All we had left were a few drunkards plucking bits of dried fruit out of their mashed potatoes.

Then the baby sneaked her way out of some broken condom. We named her Emily. I loved her and blew kissy farts on her stomach, although there was some part of me that found it hard to think of her as anything but an animated ball of dough.

What fool had told me at a dinner party that my art school dropout kitchen concoctions were good enough to pay twenty a plate for? If I saw him again, I'd pop his eye out with a wine key.

So now I was driving to Asheville for a sous chef interview at a place called Impossible Possum Bistro, with an impossibly beautiful wife and a baby in whose lumpy white face I didn't recognize a single feature of my own.

The quarry was marked with a large quartz tossed into the ditch on the far side of the road. Someone had sprayed "Dingus Crossroad" on the rock in pink spray paint.

"I told you," I said, pointing toward the rock. "See?"

I parked the car on a path that had been beaten into the woods by countless horny teenagers. Just far enough inside to hide from passing cop cars. When we pulled up, there was a blue jeep parked ahead on the path. Crumpled beer cans decorated the dirt around the tires. I turned around and looked at the baby strapped into her seat.

"I think she's ready for a nap. Let's put her under some blankets in the back."

"We aren't leaving baby in damn car."

"Okay, okay," I said. "It was a joke."

My wife handed me the baby and stood behind the car door. She dropped her shorts and panties to pull on a blue bikini. The sight of her pale bottom made me begin to swell, even in this heat. They were the kind of high, white cheeks that made everything in the world click into place for a brief second.

"Where is your suit?" she said.

"I'll swim in these," I said, "like the old days."

"Swim in jeans? Dumb old days."

I put some diapers and blankets in a yellow camping pack I had in the trunk. "I think it's back this way," I said.

I found a good-sized stick on the ground and waved it in front of me to knock any spiderwebs out of the way. It whizzed through the air. I felt as if I was the protector of my wife and infant child.

We walked through the pine trees and then out into the open field. The sky was almost painfully blue. About fifty yards off, the field was interrupted by a circle of rocks and evergreens that guarded the swimming hole. It was like an oasis that you'd see in a comic strip desert.

We placed some blankets and the baby down on a flat rock. I scratched the bottoms of her feet, and my wife popped a pacifier between her lips. We walked to the edge of the quarry, arms around each other's waists, and I slipped my thumb below her waistband to rub across the slope of her behind. Natasha lit a cigarette and stared into the quarry. It was a good thirty-foot drop.

"I not jumping in that."

"You can scamper down the side there to a ten-foot ledge."

A hot cloud of smoke blew into my face.

"Fine," I said, pulling off my shirt.

Across the gap there were a few teenagers, two guys and a girl. The boys were doing flips into the water while the girl cheered them on while looking at her phone.

"Eight point five for Aiden." I could just make out the girl shouting.

"That was a goddamn ten!"

I looked back at Natasha rubbing sunscreen on Emily's pink cheeks. I took off my shoes and stepped up to the ledge. The heat was pulling the sweat out of my skin. I tried to remember the technique for jumping thirty feet into water. I knew I had to keep my arms straight up, but I couldn't remember if I was supposed to knife my toes into the water or break the surface tension with my soles. It felt as if I was standing there for a long time, staring down into the bright blue water. The walls of the cliff still contained rectangular cuts on the otherwise smooth surface. The water below was making me thirsty.

"Get a move on, dick nut!"

Across the way, I saw one of the teenagers, a small boy with black hair, with his hands cupped around his mouth. The other one high-fived him. They were drinking beer and laughing the cheap laugh of idleness. I turned around and gave a wave to the baby and Natasha. She didn't look up from her book. I flipped off the teenagers and held it long enough to sink in, then stepped off the cliff.

The water was the same color as the sky. When I jumped in, I felt like a fly hurtling toward a bottle of Windex. The water was shockingly warm. It must have been cooking there in the Virginia sun. I let myself plunge into the warmth and held my breath, curled in a fetal ball. I looked around and couldn't see anything at all. Not a fish, rock, or weed in sight. No nature at all, only sunlight stabbing through the blue.

I stayed down there until I felt a splash in front of me and saw a stalactite of bubbles form. I rose to the surface and saw the dark-haired boy swimming toward me.

"You trying to show me up in front of my girl, old man?"

"Fuck off," I said and kicked water in his face to swim away. I was dog-paddling when his arms gripped my ribs from behind. He crawled onto my shoulders and pushed me down under the water.

I couldn't see anything except bubbles. He was on top of me, and my face was pushed against his abdomen. I tried punching him in the ribs, but the water slowed down my fists to the point where I felt like a small child trying to beat up his father.

I hit him impotently a few more times, and he let me up. His friends were whooping as he held his arms in a victory formation.

I backstroked toward my side of the cliff, watching them. There was a low ledge, and I pulled myself up. I sat there breathing for a minute. My wife was calling me, but I couldn't hear what she was saying. I coughed up a bit of water. My breath was still hard, yet I felt peaceful. A small bird hopped around the rocks in front of me. I took a warm, fist-sized rock in my hand, stood up, and chucked it at the kid's head. For a while in high school I'd been a middle reliever on the varsity team, until practice interfered with partying. But I still had my arm.

The rock glanced off his head, and the boy limply went under.

"Jayden!" the girl shouted. I looked up at her, but she didn't seem to notice me. The teenager surfaced a few seconds later, the water turning pink around his neck.

I looked up the cliff wall and began to climb. It was covered with small chips of stone that spilled down past me. The dirt stuck to my wet body. My fingers dug painfully into the rock, but I had the adrenaline of a young man pumping through me. The climb only took me a few minutes, even though I sliced open my palm on a rock. When I reached the top, Natasha and the baby were smiling in the shade.

"How is water?"

"Hot," I said.

I looked over and didn't see the other boy and girl. Only a six-pack of beer and small piles of clothes sitting on towels. I walked back to the edge and saw the two others near the water with the third. He seemed to be all right. He was sitting on a rock and cradling his head. The second boy pointed at me with his mouth open. Then he dove into the water, swimming freestyle across. He was a smooth missile in the water, like a pink barracuda. I watched him climb up, pointing and shouting at me every few feet. He had hair like wet wheat, and his body seemed to be one throbbing muscle. It was the kind of body I'd had once, before the butter, beer, and sloth turned me squishy and tired.

"Dead man!"

"What is happening?" my wife asked. She was walking toward me with a towel.

"You know. Kids," I shrugged.

I squeezed my bleeding palm into a fist so Natasha wouldn't notice. I thought about how easy it would be to toss another rock. There was even a good jagged one by my foot, but the way Natasha was looking at me felt like a warning. Like it would be a cowardly image that would sink into Emily's little brain and alter what I was to her.

Natasha handed me the towel and draped her arm over my shoulder. Her cigarette was hovering above my nipple.

"What the hell is he doing?"

I shrugged. The kid was working his way up the cliff. "Dead man!" he kept shouting.

"What you say to him?"

I could hear the little rock chips falling down the cliff as the teenager climbed.

I turned away from the kid and looked at Natasha. The sun was bright on her face. She looked frightened, and I wanted to hold her tightly and kiss her there on the ledge. Then I realized I had misjudged something. Natasha's eyes narrowed.

"Do not let him to speak like that," she said. "Beat his ass!"

Natasha glared down at the boy, her own hands curling into fists. What had seemed dreadful and unavoidable seconds before was suddenly exciting. Blood pulsed its way around my skull, getting me ready. I bent down and picked up the largest rock I could find. I could feel Natasha's eyes moving over me, perhaps seeing a new me hidden inside the old, like the nesting dolls she kept on top of our fridge.

The teenager was only about three feet from the lip.

"Go cover Emily's eyes," I said. I flexed my hand around the rock and cocked my arm back into position.

But just then, right before the moment could be completed for everyone, a gunshot whistled above the quarry. A sharp, short sound that reset the whole scene.

"Shit!" the teen said, stopping his ascent. He was just high enough to pull his head level with the ground and glance around for a second before diving back toward the other side.

Natasha's arms were wrapped tightly around my chest. "What the fuck?" she screamed. She let go and ran to Emily.

"I don't know," I said, jogging after her. "A farmer used to own this land. He would always scare us off when we came."

Natasha turned to me with yet another look on her face. "You take our baby to place farmers shoot kids?"

"I figured he was dead by now."

The teenagers had made their way up to their clothes and were running off. The dark-haired boy held his T-shirt to the back of his head.

Natasha had Emily and was marching away. I gathered up our stuff and cradled it in my arms. We had two more states to drive through, and I was dreading the rest of the ride. I followed them across the field while the teenagers sprinted past us on the other side. One of them stopped and quickly tossed a rock that whizzed past my leg, then ran to catch up with the others.

"All right," I shouted to Natasha. "You get to pick the next stop. Deal?"

A rusty ATV came rolling over the hill, driven by an old man in a blue baseball cap. Natasha stopped and I caught up with her. A cloud of dust followed the ATV down the hill. The man pulled in front of us and flipped off the motor, a .22 rifle leaning beside him.

"You the kids leaving beer cans all over the place? Think you can treat someone else's property like a garbage dump?"

"Do we look like kids?" my wife said.

The old man had the gun clutched in his hands. He started to get off of the ATV. "Wait a minute, you Steve Morris's kid?" He pulled the faded baseball cap off his head and scratched at the white hairs beneath.

"Afraid so," I said.

"Well shit, I thought so. I used to chase you off this place 'bout every month back in the day."

I tried to let out a friendly laugh. Natasha looked back and forth between us, and Emily grabbed at Natasha's long blond hair.

"Even had you in jail once. Your daddy had to come and bail you out. And now you're starting a family of your own, I see?"

"Yep."

The old man put his face in front of Emily's and stuck out his withered tongue. Emily giggled.

"Well, I hope you raise it better than your pa raised you." He laughed again, then sat back down and turned the motor on. "Do say hi to your pa when you see him."

My father had been dead for two years—done in by a heart attack in the middle of the freeway—but I smiled and said, "You bet. I'm sure he'll get a real kick out of it. I'll tell him first thing!"

Natasha and I watched him drive off and then headed back to the car. The sun was hidden by a cloud, and the temperature felt comfortably warm. I put my arm around Natasha, and she shrugged me off. I was feeling all right though, as if I had fought in a noble war and been sent home before being blown apart or disfigured for life. When we got to the car, there was a long key mark down the left side.

We strapped the baby in the back and rolled down the windows, Natasha putting another cigarette between her beautiful lips. Suddenly I remembered: Carrington Smith. That was the farmer's name, although when I had known him he'd been fat and mean, and now the years had eaten away at him until he was thin and kind. I had a lot of years to go before I got to that state though.

We pulled back onto the road. I turned up the radio and let the muggy air wash over me. I knew an ice cream and fireworks shack a half hour more down the road, if it was still there. Might be just the kind of place to take a wife and child.

SOME NOTES
ON MY BROTHER'S BRIEF TRAVELS

1.

I don't know. My little brother just got sick of town, tossed a few things in the car, and drove across the country to an old mining town in the mountains of Colorado. He drove straight there in about twenty-eight hours, stopping five times in four states for coffee and gas station sandwiches.

There isn't much else to say about that.

He got to town in the early afternoon and slept for half a day. For the next three months, he walked around photographing the dusty maws of abandoned mines.

Then he came back.

2.

The first thing my brother Foster noticed when he reached the mining town was a man in a chicken costume dancing in the late morning haze. It was a big foam costume, the full football mascot treatment. The man was holding a sign for a regional fast-food chain in one hand and flapping the other in mock flight. It was the kind of soggy, gray day you get in the mountains. Everything was covered in some kind of sad cloud.

My brother had been driving, as I've said, for twenty-eight hours, and his body had reached that special combination of no sleep, caffeine, and a stomach full of salted snacks that makes you believe it's possible you might never die. The man in the chicken costume was at an intersection where the main road turned off into a gravel road that wound up the mountain. It seemed as if the whole world might dissolve into gray for all time, then suddenly this dazzling yellow figure emerged from the fog.

You have to remember that this was during the recession, and people were taking whatever job they could get.

3.

I can't say if it was because of a girl or not. My brother and I are close in our way, but we don't talk about certain things. Neither of us is good at communicating. Foster called me once during his exodus, and I e-mailed him a few times, links to amusing news stories I'd seen or thoughts about upcoming films we were both interested in. Then, of course, I visited him near the end. My father had amassed a decent number of frequent-flier miles that were going to expire, and he had been bugging me to use them. It seemed like a good enough reason, and anyway, I myself was having issues with a woman that could only be solved by distance.

My guess is that our hometown felt used up to my brother. He had lived there his whole life. We grew up on the outskirts, moved to the center as teenagers, and he had gone to college there as well. Not me. I fled to the big city up north as soon as I could. But my brother bounced around trying to decide what to do with his life before he finally left town. It was a university town stuck in the center of North Carolina. Even growing up, there wasn't much to do except sneak into frat parties or hang out at the cafés and record stores dotting the edge of campus. What I'm trying to say is we'd already done the local college experience in high school, so I can imagine how repetitive life was starting to feel for my brother. After graduation, Foster spent the next few years trying to avoid our parents, who were still in town, and his old friends, whose successes made him feel angry and alone.

Perhaps I'm projecting.

Let's just say that he felt detached from everything. He had walked by every storefront a thousand times. The dishes at his favorite restaurants had turned into the bland, familiar taste of our mother's microwave specials. He wanted to see flat plains with horizons dotted with nothing except the occasional dinky town nestled in the dust.

I read the e-mail from my mother on my phone while I was naked and urinating. "Foster made it to Colorado," it said. "I don't think he's had a real meal in days. Can you call him? I'm worried." I was feeling tired and drained myself. I had just finished making love to my girlfriend, who had made us stop halfway through and started tearing up. She wouldn't tell me what was wrong, and then suddenly she stopped crying, stood up, and said she wanted to switch to doggy style. I asked if she was sure. We finished that way, without being able to see the other's face, and afterwards she crawled on top of me, laughing.

Nearly thirty straight hours of driving. I know there are people who can bend pieces of metal with their bare hands or live in a glass box without food for weeks. I'm not saying it's worth writing up in the newspaper, but it does make you wonder if you can ever really know a person.

4.

Five things Foster noticed on his speed tour of the United States:

a) The way Kansas is shaped, a flatness bent only by the horizon, makes it impossible not to feel alone.

b) When you emerge from the highway woods, the first sign of civilization is always a large green water tower. What do these towers do? Neither he nor I could think of any instance of them ever being used. Perhaps they weren't even full anymore, just old relics left as a reminder of leaner days.

c) The image of an orange sun slowly rising over the blue mountains of Appalachia, which my brother pulled over to photograph only an hour into his trip, has the exact unreality of an early color film.

d) The number of small mammals that survive off tourist scraps at rest stops could form an army large enough to conquer Chicago.

e) The subtle changes in fast-food architecture, especially the fake adobe walls of burger chains in the Southwest, are ripe for a postmodern cultural studies thesis—"Capitalist Simulacra in Regional Restaurant Chains" or some such. Perhaps I'll pitch a blog post about it someday.

5.

It was late at night and Foster had crossed the Mississippi River into a new state. He pulled the car into the bright parking lot of a midwestern McDonald's.

His legs felt as if they were tingling with TV static. The position of his body while driving had dug his belt into the veins of his legs for hours, cutting his circulation down to a dead man's. He limped around the parking lot to try to shake the blood back down. A couple walked by, chatting and checking their paper bag for their extra order of fries.

The streetlamps above the parking lot and the light pouring

from the glass windows were so bright, and the surrounding woods and road so dark, that the McDonald's felt like some oasis in a desert of night. You could imagine wild beasts roaming the edges of the forest, held back by a fear of the torchlike M.

Foster walked inside and went straight for the bathroom. He pissed for thirty seconds and washed his hands with a squirt of pink liquid. He had to hit the faucet button three times.

Even at this hour, there were people ahead of him in line: a couple holding each other around their waists and two teenagers talking loudly about the shapes of their boyfriends' privates.

Foster was a man of routine, part of the reason this drive was proving something about himself to himself, so he already knew his order. The cashier looked half-asleep as she punched in the different orders with fingernails that had been painted the yellow and red of the chain's logo.

Foster calculated the miles he had left to go. It seemed to him he was living a version of the American dream, staking out a new life for himself in a land miles from home. Sure, he was probably less likely to die of dysentery than travelers on the Oregon Trail, but the principle was the same.

He had two hundred dollars in his wallet and a few more in the bank.

It was his turn, and he stepped up and glanced again at the various options. He already knew what he was getting, but it was some kind of reflex. Perhaps he just didn't like looking random cashiers in the eye.

"I'll take the number six combo," he said. "With a regular Coke and large fries."

"Didn't you hear what I was saying?" the cashier said.

"What?" Foster said. Now he glanced at her. She was thin and sickly looking. Her uniform visor was turned stylishly off-center. She gave an annoyed sigh and gestured at the teen-agers, who were squirting ketchup from a hooked tube.

"No more burgers," she said. "They got the last meat!"

6.

I want to expand on something I said earlier about not knowing exactly why my brother left. Sometimes I say this to people, especially women who are strapping their bras back on, and they think it means my brother and I don't get along, or that family isn't important to me. We get along quite well. When we get together, we talk about new movies or old books, but we don't pry open our rib cages and poke at what's inside. I visit him and my parents a few times a year. The big holidays mostly.

You can lose touch with people pretty quickly this way. I remember my first girlfriend, at least the first one I'd count as real, meaning we had sex and saw each other more often than a monthly dance. Her name was Vanessa Chance, and we'd first kissed below the bleachers of a homecoming game. When the school year ended, Vanessa went away to summer camp in another state. She sent me a letter that said, "You're so far away, it's hard to believe you still exist." By that time her face was already starting to turn fuzzy in my memory. We broke up two weeks before the start of tenth grade.

7.

Foster passed the man in the chicken suit every time he drove to town. Foster didn't have a job exactly. He'd worked long hours on the fly rail of a local theater to save up for his tempo-rary escape. He was now living in an apartment he had secured on Craigslist before he drove west. His plan was to photograph all the dusty, crumbling old mines. If the photos turned out well, he would try to get a gallery to display the series alongside an artist's statement about loss, forgetfulness, and the decline of American industry. Mostly, like everyone I knew, he just wanted to pretend he was doing something with his life.

The man in the chicken suit was the first thing Foster saw every morning before getting his coffee. The man made a real impression on him. Perhaps he simply seemed so bright and absurd in the middle of this forgotten town of half-empty buildings and abandoned mines.

I wish I could say that Foster caught the man urinating behind a tree on the side of the road or with his foam head resting on a bench as he rolled strikes at a local bowling alley, but it never happened. The man just danced sluggishly on the strip of gravel on the side of the road.

Perhaps it was a woman in there or a different man each day. You couldn't tell.

8.

The town in Colorado was called Victor. I remember looking it up on Wikipedia before flying out there, and the town's population was under five hundred in the last census. I can't remember if it was named after a man named Victor or merely the concept of triumph.

9.

I was pretending to be a writer at the time, bumming around New York on meager savings, attending literary parties for free cheese cubes and sour wine. Not that things have changed on that account, beyond the cheese getting softer and the wine more delicately poured. The point is that it wasn't hard for me to make the time to visit him. I told myself it counted as research for a novel I'd been outlining over and over without ever starting.

I booked an aisle seat, so I could go to the bathroom without stumbling over some sleeping stranger. When the plane took off, the man next to me, who had the exact same haircut as my father, asked me if I wouldn't mind holding his hand until we leveled off.

"What?"

"It's just something I always do," he said. "Makes me feel calm. Normally my wife does it, but she couldn't make this trip." I didn't respond, and he started to tear up. "She has cancer," he added.

The man was balding and had a large gray mustache draped over his lip. I held his hand, which was surprisingly smooth and warm, as it would have made me feel petty and embarrassed to deny him. But I looked angrily away and imagined the nasty things I should have said to him instead.

10.

"Look," Foster said. "Right there!"

He swung the tan Camry onto the main road. The car's floor was littered with trash. I even found a petrified taco clunking around its cardboard box. It annoyed me, because the car had been my car. It was my college graduation present for my pointless degree, and I'd left it at home when I moved to the city. It wasn't worth the hassle up there. In my absence, my brother had moved in with his fast-food wrappers and Talking Heads CDs and made it his.

"Just like you said."

I turned my head in time to see the yellow blur of the man in his chicken costume. He seemed to be looking into the car at us, and I gave him a wave.

"Isn't that kind of crazy?" Foster said. "He can't be happy doing that, can he?"

11.

There wasn't a lot to do in town, and I was glad my flight was in only two days. Most of the shops sold knickknacks of the town's glory days, although how glorious those days ever were seemed up for debate.

The main things in town were the old gold mines. They were these huge jagged holes appearing suddenly off the road, like deep wounds in the land. Foster took me to three of his favorites. Each had rickety and abandoned buildings hanging over the edge of the pits. One was red, another sky blue, and the third may have once been white but now was sullied into a dusty brown. I suppose these were the buildings where the pounds of rocks had been crushed to rubble and the shiny bits separated from the dirt.

"These are really something. Can we go down in them?" We were standing over the pit by the blue building.

"Probably not a good idea," my brother said. "But we could sneak up there, maybe."

We climbed up the tower attached to the blue building. There were some dust-coated milk crates we used as seats. I couldn't see any gold glinting in the old rocks below. My brother locked a zoom lens on his camera and starting clicking away at the evergreens that dotted the hill rising beyond the pit. I halfheartedly sketched out a story idea, but mostly I sat there and tried to decide about my relationship with the woman back home or figure out if the decision had already been made for me. Every once in a while, a small bird would fly onto the railing, notice us, and flitter off again.

"It's really peaceful up here, right?" Foster said.

"Yeah," I said. "I see how someone could get used to this."

12.

"How are you doing? In life and stuff?" I was saying. There were only seven other people in the sports bar.

"Pretty good, I guess." Foster finished chewing his bite of burger. "You know, I feel like I'll give myself a few years to see if the photography takes off. If not, maybe I'll go to law school. I've been doing a little LSAT preparation already."

We finished up, and I covered the tab. It seemed like the older brother thing to do.

Walking back to the car, I saw a dark blue Ford pickup with the bright yellow chicken costume leaning against the passenger-side window. It was just the body. There was a deep black hole where the head should have been.

"Holy shit, Foster," I said, elbowing him.

We walked over and looked in through the window. The head was on the floor next to a large water bottle. It was made of bright yellow foam spray-painted with white and black for the eyes. Someone had drawn two phalluses on the dirt of the pickup's back window.

"Do you think he was eating at the bar with us?"

We went back inside and ordered another round of beers. Suddenly there was excitement in the stale bar air. We looked around. Other than the family of four eating in the corner, there were three men at the bar. They were all looking at different sports games on the overhead TVs. There was a skinny guy in a flannel shirt watching baseball, a clean-shaven teenager glued to hockey, and a slightly overweight bearded man following a golf tournament.

"With how small this town is, everyone must know the guy as the chicken suit guy," Foster whispered. "Imagine every person you pass knowing this horrible detail about you."

"Must be hell to hit on girls," I said. "Or men," I added.

When one of the men looked our way, we quickly shifted our eyes to the TV screens.

"I bet it's the beardo," I said.

We watched him eat a hot wing with surprising daintiness.

Afterwards, he carefully cleaned his fingers on a napkin. He had a small mountain of used napkins and sucked-bare bones in front of him.

"Let's go say something."

"I don't know, it could be any of them," Foster said. "Hard to tell in that suit."

We kept watching them for a while, waiting for some sign, I guess. After about forty minutes, we went home.

13.

I guess I've been thinking about my brother's trip a lot recently because I'm feeling a little lost myself. My girlfriend and I recently broke up for reasons I can't really explain. Things just fizzled out without any discernable causes. It was as if we suddenly didn't know who we were anymore, or maybe that we never realized who the other was until the end, and the realization made us simply tired instead of distraught or full of joy. We continued having sex for a few weeks, but even those close moments were spread further apart, until we went our separate ways.

Yesterday, a friend of mine—a good friend I have a hard time getting together with these days—sent out a mass e-mail announcing that he had spent the last month training to be a real estate agent. He had just that day passed his certification. Ever since I had known him, which was at least four years, he had been an aspiring actor. Now he was trading in his auditions for a burgundy blazer and not looking back. He must have mentioned this to me at some point or posted about it online, but somehow it hadn't registered, or I hadn't believed it until suddenly he was texting me to ask if I knew any couples looking for a large one-bedroom in the neighborhood next to mine.

I'm spending a lot of time alone these days. I'm trying to put my head down and get some work done. Finish up some projects and see if I can be one of the ones who pops out of the rut. Otherwise, I might have to make a right turn myself.

I'm not sure what my brother is doing right now. Last time we talked, he was still on the fence about law school. I haven't talked to him in about two months though. No particular reason. I simply haven't found the time.

WHAT YOU NEED TO KNOW ABOUT
THE WEATHERVANE

So this clown Dave buys the house next door to me, and now he's my neighbor. Okay.

It's one thing that he's a carpetbagger who thinks he can turn himself into some sort of old-fashioned, down-home country boy by wearing a cowboy hat and boots with plastic spurs. This is Virginia, mind you, not the goddamn Wild West. I don't mind. I'm a tolerant guy. But what sticks in my craw is the weathervane.

Lord knows what airplane catalog he found it in. The thing looks like it was designed by someone who was abused by farmers all his life and now gets revenge by making ugly weathervanes. It's gigantic and has some sort of southwestern theme. The rooster is painted fluorescent green with a pink beak, and it has metal ribbons that twist in the wind.

"Dave," I tell him the first day I see it. "That is one ugly son-of-a-bitch rooster."

Dave takes this as some sort of Southern joke and pats me on the back. "Looks marvelous, don't it?" he says.

Now it gets pretty windy in this part of Virginia, and the first big storm that hits, the weathervane snaps right off his roof and stabs into my front yard. Imagine if I had a daughter and she had been playing out there in a sandbox or something? She might have been decapitated by a giant rooster! How is that supposed to make me feel?

So I do the only thing I can and go out and pick up the weathervane and toss it through Dave's living room window.

Well, this Dave is a stubborn guy. I see him out there the next morning directing some Mexicans up a ladder to fix the weathervane.

"What the hell, Dave?" I say.

"Damn thing blew off and into my window in the storm," he says. "Might have to put some crazy glue on it next time. Ha ha."

Well, the next big storm that hits, what do you know? Snap, whoosh, crash. I stumble outside and pick up the rooster off the wet grass. While it technically landed in his yard this time, it's close enough to mine to make me concerned. So I march over and toss it through the jerk's dining room window.

Dave pretty much stops talking to me after that. But the weathervane goes back up, and then a few months later another big storm hits. Dave is out of town this time, and the weather-vane doesn't snap all the way, it's still half-attached and flying around in the wind like a circus flea tied to a miniature trampoline. How am I supposed to sleep knowing that any second this giant weathervane could snap off completely, fly through my bedroom window, and murder me in my own bed? I pay my taxes like anyone else. So I grab my ladder, go over to his house, and wrench off the weathervane with my hands. Then, when Dave comes back a few days later, I grab the rooster, head over to his house, ring his doorbell, and when he answers, I try to toss the damn thing through his stupid asshole heart.

Dave's a nimble fellow, and he leaps out of the way, and pretty soon I'm sitting in the county jail with a whole host of freaks and perverts. I pay my bail, return home, and what do I see as I pull in the driveway but Dave and the goddamn Mexicans reinstalling the goddamn weathervane!

I mean, I'm a man. What am I supposed to do? I've got a job on a farm outside of town. I work with my hands. These days that means pulling levers and pushing buttons on giant machines, but I try to keep some pride in my life. It's been hard lately. I've been lonely since Molly left. She was the only girl I've ever loved. I'd always thought we would be together forever, but I guess she had different plans. Every winter seems colder than the last, and the bills only get longer. And on top of all that, I have to deal with a neighbor who doesn't have an ounce of respect for me or my property? What am I supposed to do?

I just want someone to tell me what I'm supposed to god-damn do.

THINGS LEFT OUTSIDE

I wish it was me who had found her and not my husband. I kept wondering what she looked like in her natural state, so to speak. What if Gerald had moved her around?

Gerald didn't notice me when I got there. He was walking around in a semicircle as if he wanted to get closer, but her body was letting off a magnetic force that kept him away.

"Who does she belong to?" I said. I was out of breath and leaned against a tree.

"What?" Gerald said, turning around. There were a few cows nearby. They were looking at the three of us with large eyes.

"I mean, she's half on our land and half on the Smiths' pasture."

"Ah," he said. "I'm not sure it matters."

"The head is on our half," I said. "I think that should count for something."

I had been folding laundry when Gerald called. I liked doing it right when it came out, when it was so hot it almost burned my hands. I could feel his excitement through the little speaker beside my ear. Gerald told me he had been walking near the edge of our property and found our cat, Mitzy, chewing on a dead woman's face.

We'd lived on this backwoods land for two years, Gerald and I. It was a twenty-minute drive from town. If you walked through the woods, you'd come across a cow pasture cut out from the forest with rusty barbed wire. When we first moved in, we used to drink a bottle of wine and go and stick our hands through the fence so the cows would lick our palms for salt.

Gerald had already placed his bandanna over the woman's head. He said it was the Christian thing to do.

"Oh, Gerald," I said, and threw my arms around him. "Who would do something like this?"

"It's deer season," Gerald said. "She was probably shot by a hunter who realized his mistake and fled." He was looking past me. He had a large beard at that time, and his face seemed to be shrinking into it as he talked. "Yeah," he said. "That's probably what happened."

The woman was on her belly beneath the barbed wire, legs jutting into the cow pasture. You could tell by the color of the dirt that there had been a lot of blood, yet her jeans and green button-up looked untouched from the back. They could have been pulled fresh out of the dryer.

"I think I have that exact same shirt," I said. "I bought it on sale at Gap."

I squatted close to the body. I thought she would look peaceful, and that I would feel a spiritual calm spread through my veins, but it didn't happen. With her head hidden under the bandanna, she looked more like a mannequin. I wanted to reach out and bend her limbs into a livelier pose.

Gerald squeezed my collarbone with his hands. He bent down and put his dry lips against my cheek. "The cops said they'd be here soon." He said it so matter-of-factly. She was already passing out of our hands. "We should go back to the house."

"No," I said. "We need to be with her till they come."

My husband sighed and sat on a stump with his hands on his knees. I stayed in the damp grass near the body. The woman was laying belly down, with her arms curled in front of her head. I could imagine sleeping like that, with a pillow under my head instead of mud. I kept hoping the wind would blow the bandanna off her head. There were a few bugs crawling over her body. One flew onto my foot, and I flicked it away.

"I'm getting kind of hungry," Gerald said after a bit.

Not much normally interrupted our eating out here. We inherited the house from Gerald's parents after his father died of a stroke and his mother gave up and moved to Florida. It was a quiet place, but close enough to town that we weren't hillbilly hermits.

Gerald and I had met in high school. He had been on the state champion football team, although I always forgot which position. We'd been together for long enough it felt like nothing at all.

It was already getting dark when the police arrived. They turned the forest upside down with lamps and walkie-talkies. They took Gerald aside, and I couldn't hear what he was saying. He seemed to be giving a description of our cat.

I watched the police dump out the woman's backpack. There was a bag of trail mix, three tubes of beauty product, a bottle of red wine, and a digital camera. All objects I own and use myself. They put these in plastic bags that they zipped shut. At one point I thought I saw Mitzy, her eyes bouncing beneath a bush like glow-in-the-dark balls.

The police only asked me if I'd heard any unusual noises. I said no, and they said they might need to talk to me down the road.

After that we had to leave the area.

• • •

When we got home, I went to the bathroom. I flushed the toilet and then looked in the mirror and tried to cry. I walked around the house, calling for Mitzy. She kept darting under different pieces of furniture.

Gerald was snacking in front of the TV. I sat down next to him and took a handful of chips.

"Was she beautiful?" I asked.

"What? I didn't know her," he said quickly.

"But you saw her face before you covered it up," I said. "What did she look like?"

"Christ, Carol. I dunno. Normal?"

"That's it?" I said. "You don't remember her eye color or anything?"

Gerald stood up and walked over to the trash can and spat out a plum pit, then walked back and sat down.

"She had brown hair," he said. "About your length. I dunno if you'd call her pretty. Pretty enough I guess. Her face was wide open and stuck in the mud. I didn't want to keep looking at her eyes."

"For some reason I want her to be beautiful," I said.

I could have been doing anything when it happened. Slicing an apple, napping on the porch, wrapping my fingers around Gerald's privates. And out there, she was breathing her last breaths. The police had taken the body away in a dark bag, but I kept wondering about her. I would try to imagine her face, and it would be the face of a sister of mine. A twin sister I never knew I had, a mirror reflection I had failed to protect.

I didn't dream about her, or didn't remember the dreams, but I also didn't sleep much. I rolled onto my side and watched a small pool of saliva leak out of Gerald's red mouth.

At breakfast, I couldn't help myself. "Would you say she was older or younger than me?"

Gerald was dipping pieces of bread into his runny eggs. He took the piece that was halfway in his mouth and placed it down on the rim of the plate.

"It's in the past," he said. "Death is just a part of life. I think we should let it go and move on." He put the toast back into his mouth. I got up to refill my coffee.

It was a bright day outside. A ladybug flew into the window. I thought I heard gunshots in the distance.

"Hey, maybe we could go in and see a movie later tonight," Gerald said. He scraped a large chunk of butter across his toast. "Wouldn't that be fun?"

"Her skin was pale. It seemed like she might have a lot of freckles, like me," I said. "Do you remember her freckles?"

"Christ," Gerald said. "Sometimes I wish we'd never even found that thing."

Since the economy had gone sour, Gerald hadn't had much work. He got a call every now and then to fix up a rotted porch or help build a new staircase, but most days he sat around. That day, he put on his coat and gloves and drove off like it was any other Tuesday. He'd finished up his breakfast while I was in the shower.

"Gonna go put in some applications," he said. "You never know when things will pick up."

Mitzy came out from behind the stove and jumped on my lap. I ran my fingers over her head a few times. "You weren't really chewing her face, were you? You were just licking it clean to get a good look."

I listened to Gerald's pickup sputter off, then walked over to my jacket and pulled out the policeman's card. I told the lady who answered my name and said I wanted to know what they had learned. "Did the autopsy reveal anything? Has anyone identified the body? Do they have to do that before the autopsy?"

"I'm sorry, ma'am," she said. "That's privileged information. We can't give out information on ongoing investigations to anyone who isn't a relative of the victim."

"How do I know if I'm family or not if you can't tell me her name?"

"I'm sorry, you'll have to wait for the public announcements same as everyone else."

Mitzy yawned and hopped off my lap to find her bowl of water.

"The secret to a good red sauce is brown sugar," Margaret said. "You might not think it, but that's what all the restaurants do. Mix it in until it's muddy and mix in the noodles."

We were drinking vodka cranberries on her porch. I'd decided to get off the property, sit somewhere where I didn't feel the presence of the spot by the fence.

"I used to use powdered sugar, but it always tasted like some trash from Olive Garden." She gave a laugh. Margaret liked to repeat the tricks she'd learned on cooking shows. I waited for a lull to release my secret.

"Margaret, we found a dead woman on our land," I said, taking her hand as if to protect her. "She was by herself and bleeding all over the ground. The killer is still out there."

I waited for her shock.

"I know, isn't it awful? You poor darling."

I pulled back. "How did you know?" I'd been watching the local news every night and hadn't heard a peep.

"Gerald told me. Raj and I ran into him at the store." Margaret took a sip from her drink. The cranberry juice left a thin red sheen above her lips. "What can you do, though? Last week Asha's goldfish went belly up, and she woke us up screaming. She was in our bedroom doorway with the sad,

slimy thing in her hands. Just have to put it out of your mind,
I guess."

There were a lot of paths in the woods. I kept thinking someone
would spring out from behind a hill or oak and twist a knife into
my stomach. I picked up a large stick to walk with. There was
a chunk of wetness around the top, some fungus or mold, and I
dropped it back down.

When it was Gerald's turn to pick our movies, he always
chose detective films. His favorites were the French ones that
were filmed in such dark shadows that you'd think the sun never
flew over Paris. I never quite understood them, but Gerald would
squeeze the popcorn in his fists into tight wads of excitement.
And yet here I was scouting the woods alone.

The spot seemed all wrong without the body. Even though
I had visited that corner of the pasture dozens of times, nothing looked right. The barbed wire was spaced too far apart, and
the trees had been moved a few inches to the left. I stepped on
a small plant with foreign-looking leaves.

I walked around stooped over until my back hurt. I didn't
find any clues. Even the bloodstain seemed to have been soaked
up by the dirt.

There was something peaceful about the spot though. I went
home and packed a small lunch and came back with a blanket
and a book. After a time, Mitzy came by and jumped on my
lap. Together we dozed off and woke only when Gerald's truck
pulled into the driveway.

Gerald peeled off his undershirt and approached me in bed. His
beard glistened with flecks of water from the sink. We had the
window open, and the wind moved over my face and shoulders. Mitzy watched us from the foot of the bed. When Gerald's

fingers landed on my neck, I rolled myself onto him. Gerald was silent as I grunted. Something had been welling up inside me, and I let it out until we returned to our sides of the bed covered in a sheen of sweat.

"Well sure, I could be over there in an hour," Gerald said.

"What's happening?" I said. "Was that the police?" It was two o'clock in the afternoon, and we'd been playing cards on the living room table.

"It was Wallace Smith."

"Oh my god, *Wallace*? He did it?" Wallace was our neighbor who owned the farm the body was half on.

"What?" Gerald said. "Wallace wants me to help reshingle his barn roof." He smiled and got his measuring tape out of the top drawer. He pulled it out a few inches and let it snap back. "I guess he heard about my employment status. 'Neighbors help neighbors; that's what we do' was how he put it. Funny guy."

It didn't sound right. Wallace Smith had never called Gerald for any help before. In fact, when we'd first moved in, we had a big dispute over the land boundary. For a while we thought we were going to have to hire a lawyer.

"What if he thinks you know something?" I said.

"I know a lot about roofing. That's why he's hiring me."

"No, Gerald, about the *murder*."

"Murder?" he said. "Are you still on about that? Wallace is just a nice old man who needs a hand. I think he got an arm twisted under a tractor or something. But don't worry, I'll be careful." He winked and gave me a kiss on the cheek. "It'll be nice to have a little extra cash flowing in, eh? Maybe we can see that movie."

· · ·

Margaret was insisting I try a new Thai restaurant with her in town. She said I needed to breathe some city air. I was afraid something would happen, and I would miss it.

"Gerald," I said, "do you know where my shirt is?"

"What shirt?" He was shouting but standing only in the other room.

"My green blouse. The button-up one with the pockets from Gap."

Gerald walked around the corner. He had Mitzy in his arms and was pulling back her ears. He shrugged. "If it was stained, I probably threw it in the wash."

On one path, I found a candy bar still in its shiny wrapper. On another, three crumpled beer cans and a full pack of cigarettes, which looked like hunter trash. It was almost cold in the shade of the woods. All the bugs and animals were hiding from me.

I went back to the spot. I placed my hands carefully between the barbs of the fence and maneuvered into the cow pasture. A barb caught my thigh and ripped a hole on the way down. I could feel a trickle of blood dampening the denim. There were a few footprints in the mud and cow pies. They led in different directions. A cow wandered over and licked my hand with a rough, pink tongue.

The pasture was a few hundred feet long. At the end of it I could see the Smiths' barn. The only thing on the roof was a rusty weathervane. Had Gerald lied to me? What was he doing instead of roofing?

I thought I could follow the line of trees on the far side along the barbed wire without being seen. When I got close, I crouched behind a row of hedges and listened to Gerald and Wallace Smith laughing. Gerald had something in a blue tarp about the size of a body draped over his shoulder.

"Just hurry with it if you want to get paid," Wallace was saying. I was trying to breathe as quietly as possible, and it was hurting my lungs.

Gerald and Wallace went around to the door of the barn, and I squeezed my way between the fence slats. "Fuck, this shit is heavy," Gerald said.

I thought about all the little moments in my life that had brought me to this moment and how pointless they all seemed. A brown chicken walked around the side of the barn, and I tried to shoo it off. It moved closer, bobbing its head. It seemed to be staring me right in the face.

"Carol?"

I looked up. Gerald had materialized on the roof. The rolled-up tarp was at his feet. He held a hand over his eyes to gaze down at me, making his face pitch black.

"What are you doing down there?" he said. He had a big smile sliced into the center of his beard. The sun was shining hard on him.

"Who's there?" someone said. Then Wallace hobbled around the side of the barn. "Why if it isn't a pretty lady," he said. He reached out with his good hand. The other was limp in a sling. "How are you, Carol? I didn't expect to see you again so soon."

"I was just out for a walk," I said. I could feel my heart thumping impotently against my chest. "How's the roofing?"

"Coming along," Gerald shouted down. "Hot day, though. If you're walking back through, could you bring me a glass of lemonade?"

I found it harder and harder to talk to Gerald. He would come home sore and hungry and ready for the TV. We would eat dinner, make love or not make love, then go to sleep. I stopped asking him about Wallace or the body. The roofing job went on and on.

When his snores started, I slid out of bed and searched through his clothes. There was nothing unusual, only some movie ticket stubs. I didn't know what clues I was supposed to be putting together.

The corner of the fence was still a quiet place for me. I would go there to read and think. I rubbed the dark veins creeping up my calves. I could calculate only a year or two before we'd probably want to add a child. Life settled into its mold no matter what you did.

It was getting close to dusk. I went over to the fence and ran my fingernail over the rusty wire. Gerald was off hammering nails into something with Wallace. It was a quiet day, and the clouds knocked into each other in the sky. I stood in front of the fence and got on my knees and scooted in backwards. My arms were out in front of me. The mud was cold against my face.

I didn't think about a lot of things. Or I did, but in a detached way, as if they were slowly trickling out of my mind.

I felt comfortable, you could even say at peace, and lay there in the mud for a long time.

Out of the corner of my eye, I thought I saw Mitzy. She darted behind an oak tree and hissed loudly. With one ear in the mud it was hard to hear, but one or possibly two sets of boots were approaching.

FAMILIAR CREATURES

LAWN DAD

Some nights Dad would come home with the demon on his
breath and topple right over in the yard. Momma would
have to tug on him till he came inside so the neighbors wouldn't
start yapping.

One night she didn't even bother waiting up, and he was left
out there on the lawn. He woke up the next day to the crunch-
crunching of the garbage men. I was running to meet friends at
the pool and almost tripped over his legs.

"Can you believe it, Luanne? Your momma's abandoned me."
He was weeping into a handful of dandelions.

I could see the neighbors' silhouettes watching us from
behind their curtains. Momma had told me not to help him, but
he grabbed at my ankle, so I gave him my lunch. It was only
baloney and swiss anyway.

When I got home, Dad was still sprawled out on the front
lawn as if he was trying to make a snow angel out of grass. The
neighbors were peeping through holes in the fence.

"I married a damn fool," Momma said. "He can rot out there
for all I care."

I sneaked him a pack of crackers later. He was bunched up
in the dark like a pile of leaves. Up close, I noticed his face was
scrunched in pain.

"Luanne, love eats away at you like a colony of termites,"
he said.

I told him he should move inside, that he was liable to melt away in this heat, but he said the woman inside was not the same woman he married, and that was a terrifying thing.

Dad stayed there all summer. Momma wouldn't talk to him, just smoked cigarettes and glared at him through the window. I was sneaking out the back door to see Bobby Jackson that summer. He had a bright yellow motorbike and took me anywhere I wanted to go. One night, Bobby put his hands under my shirt and said we'd never be apart. I skipped right across the yard forgetting Dad was there. He was scowling as Bobby rode away through the night. In the weak glow of the streetlamps, Dad's face looked thin and green.

Finally, Momma went outside and grabbed his arm. "All right," she said, "we have our differences, but who doesn't? I think we can start again."

"I fear it's too late," he said. When Momma tugged on his arm, he screamed in pain. The grass had already grown up through his skin. His roots had taken hold, and I had stopped bringing him food weeks before.

Slowly his body grew softer and greener until it split apart into the lawn. Momma cried a lot in the bathroom with the tub running. Fall crept up on us, and the summer was done.

Now Dad was just a thick clump in the dirt. I kneeled next to him and put down my ear. "Promise me you'll keep me nice and trim," the wind whispered through the blades. I didn't think he could hear me anymore, but I said I would.

I mow lawns all around the neighborhood now. I have a shiny, red mower I can spin around on a dime. I charge exactly ten dollars a yard.

MY LIFE IN THE BELLIES OF BEASTS

I was born prematurely and, as such, was a very small child. So small, in fact, that shortly after emerging into the world, I was gobbled up by a clever fox that terrorized my parents' farm. It had sneaked in the back door while everyone was distracted. My mother's tears of joy turned acid, and my father cursed the lazy farmhand he'd tasked with mending the fence. These were the first and last words I ever heard my parents utter.

It was cozy and warm inside the fox's belly. I barely noticed what had happened. To me, it seemed I had merely gone from one womb to another. When I was hungry, I ate the scraps of raw meat that fell around me. When I was sad and wailed, the fox howled lullabies to guide me back to sleep. All in all, my early days were bearable.

In time, I began to grow skittish. I was no longer a baby, and I needed to stretch my limbs. One day, as if to answer my prayers, the fox was cornered by a local hunter and his giant mastiffs. The fox tried to run away, but I had grown so large that I weighed her down, and she was torn apart by the hounds. I felt the cool air and saw the harsh sunlight for the first time before being swallowed by the largest dog.

I can't deny I felt a great sadness as I settled among the bits of organ and clumps of fox fur. Yes, the fox had kidnapped me, but she had also been my home, and that is never an easy thing to lose.

Still, the mastiff was roomier and more appropriate for a growing boy. I could feel my muscles developing as I did push-ups on the soft stomach floor and pull-ups on the outline of the mastiff's large spine. When the dog bounded through the grassy fields, I would crawl up his throat and rest my chin on the back of his massive tongue, gazing out at the dry, open world.

I even fell in love this way, believe it or not. There was a kind girl who lived next to the hunter's house who would feed the mastiff I lived in tasty leftovers through the gaps in the fence. She wore pastel sundresses and had dandelions in her hair. I couldn't believe how light and beautiful she looked in the sun.

"What are you doing in there?" the girl said when she saw me peeking from the back of the mouth.

"I live down here," I said, ashamed.

"Well, come on out!"

She laughed, but I was afraid and slid back down into the guts. I didn't think a boy who had lived his life in the bellies of beasts was worthy of her.

I howled with self-pity, and the girl rubbed the mastiff's belly, saying, "There, there."

Eventually my constant loneliness made me resolve to leave the dog's belly. And I did. Using all my strength, I pulled my way out of the mastiff's maw. It was dark outside the dog. My limbs ached, and I decided to rest. As I sat on squishy ground, I realized I was merely in another belly. The dog had been gobbled up by a grizzly bear when I hadn't been paying attention. I couldn't believe my bad luck!

When I tried to escape the bear, she grew angry and climbed up a tall tree. I was almost a teenager now, and life felt like a rotten trap. Everything that seemed sweet contained hidden thorns. If I had fresh honey in my grasp, it was followed by the painful sting of swallowed bees.

But life moves on, and one grows accustomed to anything. Years passed. The grizzly was drugged and placed on a boat that set off for a foreign zoo. The boat was caught in a terrible storm, and the bear and I were tossed overboard, only to be consumed by a shark that was later swallowed, accidentally, by a giant sperm whale.

I was now in the largest belly I had ever been in. There was nothing to restrain me anymore. I was a man, and I had to make a life for myself. I set to work, building a shelter out of driftwood scraps and skewering fish from the stomach's pond for food. Sometimes I thought about the little girl in the sundress and felt a sadness in my stomach. I lived in the whale for a long time. My skin grew spots, and my hair fell softly to the ground. My years were swallowed one by one by the beast of time.

Then one day, I noticed the whale was no longer moving. I hadn't felt stillness in many years. I was afraid and sat waist deep in the cold saltwater. I pressed my ear to the whale's rib cage and heard shouts and noises beyond the barrier of flesh. Then metal claws tore the walls of my world open, and I tumbled onto a wooden deck.

It took my eyes quite some time to adjust to the light. My old skin was covered in flecks of blood and slick blubber.

Between the unshaven sailors, I saw a woman looking at me and smiling. Her skin was crumpled with age, and her hair was long and white. She was wearing a green sundress and holding out her hand.

"How did you find me?" I managed to say.

"I've been searching for you all my life," she said. She bent down to kiss me softly on the brow.

She helped me off the ship's floor and gave me a bowl of hot soup. The sailors waved good-bye to us at the next port. We married and bought a little apartment in the city, far away from the woods and wild beasts. Inside, we enveloped each other in our arms and whispered the words we'd saved up over all that time. There weren't many years left for us, so we were determined to live them happily. We drank dark wine and filled our bellies with rich meals of liver and ripe fruit.

Time passed, and my days were calm.

Yet despite all my happiness, life was uneasy for me on the outside. Often at night I would wake up in a sweat, my body encased in the tight sheets of our little bed in a cold apartment in a city surrounded by the warm sea. I felt small and alone in that dark room. I could feel the breath of my wife on my neck, but it felt like the breath of some unstoppable and infinitely large beast, the one waiting for the day that it would swallow me inside the blackness of its belly forever.

THE SOLDIER

The soldier was called into the sergeant's tent and slapped across the face. There was something the soldier had done, of course, but he wasn't sure what. The sergeant was yelling at the soldier, about either the shine or lack of shine on the toes of the soldier's boots. It was a hot day in that foreign land. The soldier left the sergeant's tent and, with the sting still blooming on his cheek, kicked a mangy dog in the ribs.

I would like to make a point here about violence inflicted on one person being passed down to another in an endless cycle. But the kick was accidental. The soldier was running to hide the tears welling in his eyes and didn't notice the dog in his path. The soldier was far from home. He was in a lonely place, and the men he was trying to kill always seemed to be hiding in large bushes where he couldn't see them.

The dog, however, was not far from home. He was a native dog and so was considered an enemy by the other soldiers. When the dog came by begging, the soldiers threw their empty bottles and cigarette butts at him. The dog would then run back into the forest only to come upon the rebel camp. There, the rebels, believing the black-haired dog to be an evil omen, would hit him and yank his tail.

The dog spent the days of the war like that, running to and from the camps, always in search of companionship. The soldier stepped on a land mine, and the sergeant died of an exotic disease, but the dog was still there. There were no other dogs in the woods he ran through. When he was hungry, he sat on the ground and gnawed on his own leg. Sometimes at night he would see the face of the man in the moon and bark loudly in anger.

THE HEAD BODYGUARD HOLDS HIS HEAD
IN HIS HANDS

When the Dictator settles on a day of shopping, the head bodyguard notifies the store twenty minutes in advance. In this way, assassination plots are eluded. The Dictator arrives in a black limousine along with his four favorite bodyguards. The head bodyguard sits in the front seat and lazily scans the tops of buildings for any glints that might signify a sniper rifle or bazooka. The Dictator reclines in the backseat between two of the other bodyguards—two brothers, in fact—and sips a small cup of single malt Scotch and water. Sometimes he will substitute the Scotch for an obscure brand of grape soda he has consumed since childhood, although only if the Dictator thinks that the bodyguards will not be able to guess the contents of his drink. This is why the Dictator only drinks from black mugs.

Hastily, the boutique has been emptied until only one female employee remains. It is well known that the Dictator is fond of well-breasted women, and indeed the woman in the red dress— for the Dictator prefers red dresses on well-breasted women— is the bustiest woman the store currently employs.

The head bodyguard has known the three other bodyguards for as long as he can remember. Their fathers were junior partners in the same law firm, and they spent their summers exercising at the same country club gym. As schoolboys, their physiques and large allowances allowed them to twist and punch the arms and legs of smaller, poorer boys in the hallway between classes.

The head bodyguard has also known the Dictator for decades. By now, he feels the inevitable affection that results from years of proximity.

The bodyguards wear black Italian leather jackets, black sunglasses, and black slacks, and each carries a black snakeskin briefcase that contains various items the Dictator may or may not require. Each briefcase's contents are unique. The head bodyguard's briefcase contains the Dictator's honorary diplomas—for the Dictator never completed university work on his own, having dropped out to pursue a career in advertising—an address book of various allies and surrogates of the Dictator; a list of the Dictator's enemies, alongside each of their greatest weaknesses; a small box of ammunition; and two gold-plated .38 caliber pistols.

The Dictator stands at five foot seven, three inches below the national average, and has the vague sort of face that, if seen in a group photo, requires an extra second to place. In the store, the Dictator does not browse. Instead, he reclines on a white leather couch while the large-breasted woman parades the latest designs in front of him. The three other bodyguards stay in the store with the Dictator while the head bodyguard stands watch out front. This is the job the head bodyguard prefers, as it allows him to smoke his hand-rolled cigarettes and not deal with any fits the Dictator might have if the clothes do not fit him correctly. The head bodyguard takes a long drag of his cigarette and feels his chest fill up with scratching heat. He exhales into the face of a large woman carrying a small dog in her purse. Move along, the head bodyguard says, gesturing with his head. The head bodyguard takes off his jacket and drapes it over his arm. It is summer.

Inside the store, the other bodyguards nod along with the large-breasted woman at the outfits the Dictator has picked out. The Dictator carries a black credit card issued specially for him by the Minister of the Treasury, and when he pays for his clothes, he likes to say, Put it on the people's tab. A little joke. Today he is wearing a tightly tailored gray and purple pinstriped suit, ostrich skin shoes, silver cuff links shaped like roaring lion heads, and a bright yellow tie printed with ionic columns. Since assuming power, the Dictator has always clad himself in the most fashionable of modern garb. He says that this is to inspire the people, although the head bodyguard secretly thinks it is a compensation for the Dictator's otherwise forgettable appearance.

When he was a little boy, the head bodyguard once held the Dictator's head in the bottom of a toilet for a full two minutes while two other boys flipped the flush lever and punched the Dictator in his stomach.

The Dictator, for his part, remembers every bruise and noogie and night spent crying to his sickly mother about the bullies at school. After the Dictator assumed power—through a series of title changes, departmental merges, and power transfers that left the public completely confused as to who was in charge until the Dictator interjected his face on every billboard and screen—he tracked down the bullies who had tormented his school years. When he discovered that one of his most persistent tormentors had broken his neck in a freak hang gliding accident, the Dictator was furious. He crushed two rusty antique iron thumbscrews on his palace floor. Still, he succeeded in locating four of the most memorable bullies, and these he hired as his personal bodyguards.

The shouting of the Dictator, who is enraged that a certain pair of pants—one that contains real silver woven through the fabric—do not come in his size, fades through the walls and glass and into the ear of the head bodyguard as if descending on him from some great height. The head bodyguard would not consider himself a philosophical man. He dropped out of college in his second year to begin his short-lived sport-fishing career, which resulted in three sunken boats and one lawsuit, before being hired by the Dictator. Leaning against the large glass window, smoking his hand-rolled cigarette, and watching the awkward bodies of the city's residents avoid each other on the sidewalk, the head bodyguard begins to wonder about his role. He is a bodyguard, and thus his job is to protect the physical body of the Dictator from outside harm. But what about harm that the Dictator causes to himself? The Dictator has been known, in moments of anger, to pound his hands against the wall, yet if the head bodyguard tries to restrain the Dictator, his hands will be bitten by the Dictator's nubby teeth, for the Dictator grinds his teeth constantly in the night with a squeaking that at first kept the head bodyguard awake but now lulls him like a painful lullaby. Those teeth are a part of the Dictator's body, of course, yet the head bodyguard does nothing to stop their erosion. Is this a failure of his charge? And even then, does his duty end entirely with the physical body of the Dictator? Is it not also, in some sense, his duty to protect the mind of the Dictator from corruption? These and other thoughts stumble around the head bodyguard's head until the Dictator, trailed by the three other bodyguards, kicks open the door, either in anger or in imitation of the Western the five of them watched together last night.

Gathering a small crowd of women and children shoppers, the Dictator presents a short speech. There are times of fear and there are times of action, he tells the crowd, and as a man of action, he will act and act fearlessly to complete the actions that are required of him. Several people clap and hold out their ID cards for the Dictator to sign, which he does. The people clap again as the Dictator and his bodyguards get into the black limousine and drive off with the windows rolled up. The small crowd stands around for a few seconds, then disperses.

The Dictator is guarded at all times by at least one bodyguard, except when he is sleeping in his massive canopy bed or bathing in his only slightly less massive claw-foot tub. The life of the Dictator is essential to the health of the state, and no chances can be taken. When he goes to the toilet, one bodyguard will lean against the bathroom sink and hand the Dictator any reading material he desires. The Dictator has long believed that images of nude bodies bound to furniture with ropes can ease bowel movements. When the Dictator is feeling amorous, he will have a guard bring the first lady, and he will perform the carnal act in the guard's presence. The head bodyguard is nervous today, knowing that a set of new designer clothes inflates the Dictator's libido. Sometimes the Dictator wishes to try an acrobatic position that requires two or more guards to hold the first lady in the air and guide the Dictator's movements. Often the head bodyguard notices the Dictator staring at him when he orgasms into the first lady. The Dictator's eyes perform a quick twitching moment right at climax, and his upper lip begins to curl. This unsettles the head bodyguard, whose parents fought often in his presence and who has long struggled with intimacy.

Driving home from the store, the head bodyguard cannot help but notice several messages spray-painted in shaky letters along the walls of buildings. The head bodyguard does not pay attention to politics. He was raised from a young age to never talk about politics or religion, and he certainly does not talk about either one with the Dictator on their strolls through the manicured gardens. The messages list a certain date, but it is a date the head bodyguard does not remember. Perhaps it is a future date that has yet to occur. Perhaps the date's meaning will be clear only then.

When the Dictator returns to his mansion, the head bodyguard walks quickly to the compound's coop and then returns to the house with two live chickens squawking in his hands. The Dictator comes outside, and together they walk to the moat. Once there, the head bodyguard hands the chickens to the Dictator, who launches them, one at a time, toward the yawning jaws of his alligators. The feeding of the alligators always visibly excites the Dictator, who paces around the moat as the alligators sink back into the muddy water, wet white feathers dangling from their lips. It is typically after feeding the alligators that the Dictator has intercourse with his wife, so when the Dictator heads back inside, the head bodyguard rolls a cigarette and remains.

The head bodyguard carries two automatic pistols, one tucked into the shaft of his right leather boot, the other stuck into his left armpit. The head bodyguard is unsure what the Dictator carries beyond the six-inch blade sheathed along the side of his personal briefcase. The Dictator's gun cabinet contains at least two-dozen firearms, including a silver-lined .44 Magnum, its handle engraved with a lion tearing into the flank of a unicorn—the Dictator's personal crest. One time, the head bodyguard walked into the Dictator's study and found him half-naked, sobbing, and carefully cleaning the Magnum's cylinders with Q-tips and hydrogen peroxide.

Finishing his cigarette, the head bodyguard stretches his arms and legs. Through the muddy water, he can see the black shadows of the alligators twisting. Even though the head bodyguard is aware that he is surrounded by a 25,000-volt electric fence, monitored by twelve closed-circuit cameras, and standing next to a man-made moat, there is something about the arranged foliage that gives the head bodyguard a sense of being at peace with nature.

When the head bodyguard returns to the mansion, the Dictator has retired for the night. One of the other bodyguards is in the shower washing various fluids out of his hair while another drops a few soiled items into the washing machine and presses start. It is at this time that the four bodyguards can relax and discuss their bodyguard duties with each other at leisure. The last bodyguard has cracked open a few bottles of the Dictator's imported Château Duras. The bodyguards hang their black coats over the backs of their chairs. They remove their black sunglasses, put down their black briefcases, kick off their black shoes, and wiggle their black-socked toes. The bodyguards play their cards and drink their wine, hunched over in their wooden chairs. They drink the red wine in gulps. The night grows long.

Although a short and almost unnoticeable man when face-to-face, it is after the Dictator has departed that his presence is felt most strongly. While the Dictator has retired for the night, the bodyguards have a slight nervousness in their eyes as they play cards. Every now and then, one of the bodyguards twists his head and hops slightly from his chair, as if a command has been barked only to him, before sitting back down and taking another gulp of wine.

The head bodyguard has not watched the news in many years. He wonders just what it is that the Dictator does. What does he govern? What enemies stalk him in the night? When the first bullet is fired, which of the four bodyguards will leap into its path? While the head bodyguard is pondering these questions, the youngest bodyguard gets drunker and angrier.

He has emptied a bottle and a half of wine himself, and his face has grown as red as the woman's red dress. He bangs his fists on the table. He says he can no longer be a party to the Dictator, whom he calls the little twerp, making the head bodyguard cringe reflexively. The youngest bodyguard says the people are angry, and it will only be so long before these angry people put bullets into the Dictator and each and every bodyguard. Well, I'm not going to take a bullet for a kid who cried every time he got a wedgie, the youngest bodyguard says, and leaps up with his gun already in his hand.

Instantly, the head bodyguard's training takes over. He whips his own chair from under his behind and knocks the gun out of the youngest bodyguard's hand. The other two body-guards join in. The four descend on each other as they used to do to boys on the dusty playground of their high school. With each punch, the head bodyguard is transported back to that innocent place.

All the crashing and yelling awakens the Dictator. He lies awake in bed staring at the door. His room is completely black, and he pulls the silk covers tightly over his face. There are many people who want to kill him, and he imagines each and every one working their way up the stairs. Thousands of imag-inary feet march up the staircase of his mind. After a minute, the Dictator shouts down to the bodyguards.

Sir, please go back to sleep, the head bodyguard shouts back. We are only fighting over the inestimable honor of being the first bodyguard to accept your assassination bullet.

THE MAYOR'S PLAN

The new mayor thinks it would be good publicity to give out keys to the city to distinguished citizens. Not real keys of course—the gates to the city were torn down a long time ago—but gold-plated hunks of metal that have to be carried with two hands.

The mayor is a popular mayor, and his keys become popular items among businessmen, politicians, architects, and the like. The mayor gives out more and more keys, until soon they became de rigueur for any respectable member of high society.

I work down at the key factory. All day long I hammer away at those shiny lumps. I live in the old meatpacking zone in what used to be a slaughterhouse. Every morning I take the bus across town to the factory. Along the way, I watch the latest buildings shoot up like weeds. The city is booming, and sometimes heading home, I look around and don't even know where I am.

But, as is the nature of things, the mayor's popularity doesn't last. There's a scandal about misappropriated funds used to produce the keys and rumors of an illegitimate child. To keep up his popularity, the mayor increases the order for keys tenfold. He begins to award keys to all the wealthy and popular residents, then to all the artists and musicians of any stripe, and finally to anyone with full-time employment. Soon the mayor's assistants set up a stand on Main Street and hand out the keys to anyone with proper ID. Everyone in the city has always felt they were special, and now they have a symbol to prove it.

The output at the factory is crazy. We're popping them out like popcorn. To cut down on expenses, the mayor made us switch to fool's gold, which glints just the same. I return home at midnight, my hands cracked and splintered by shards of fake gold. It's winter, and my radiator is broken. I sleep shaking in the cold. In my dreams, thin golden planes plummet through lock-shaped clouds toward the earth.

I don't know the mayor, and I'm not sure if the keys are saving his job. I do know that everyone I meet seems angry. They yell at each other on the streets over whose key is bigger or brighter. People carry their keys around and use them to knock others out of their path on the subway. Just yesterday I myself was mugged by two youths who held me against a wall with a shaft of fool's gold pressed into my neck.

What has the city come to?

Recently the mayor announced a new plan to address the social unrest. He has worked with several top designers to come up with a beautiful bow that will be dispensed to the citizens and when worn will display one's love of the city. I've already seen a few at the unemployment office. They're a dazzling blue.

COLONY

I received my acceptance to the colony in the mail. Or rather my husband had laid it out for me when I got home. The letter said I should be proud of my acceptance, and that almost no one, or at any rate very few, was chosen.

The letter suggested I get my life in order so that I could come to the colony as soon as possible. I suppose it was just an odd way of phrasing, "get your life in order," perhaps a phrasing that showed the artistic leanings of the colony.

"Good," my husband said. "It will be good to have some time apart." My husband was in the process of becoming my ex-husband. He was very eager to affix that prefix.

"But I haven't worked on anything in a long time."

"And now you will," my husband said. He reminded me that I had that project I always talked about, the project I had applied with.

He stood up and extended his arms so that his hands alighted on my shoulders. "I'm glad. I'm glad for you."

I arrived at the colony by taxi. It was fall, and the trees were either bare or covered in yellow and red leaves. The colony consisted of two barns, one white and one gray. The barns and much of the woods had been owned by an artist famous in these parts. She had thrown, I read in the acceptance letter, a large number of scandalous parties in the field down through the woods. I was allowed to visit the field, as long as I remembered to carry a pass.

I was late, and the director of the colony met me in the driveway. She had her car door already open.

"The first barn is where you sleep and eat," the director of the colony told me, pointing at the large white barn. Then she pivoted and pointed at an equally large gray barn. "The second barn is where you work."

In addition to myself, there were five other residents at the colony. According to the director, we had all been selected from a large pool by a rigorous process.

"We encourage you to spend your time working, not socializing," the director said. "You don't have to interact with any of the other residents unless both you and they want to. And I won't be around."

"I understand," I said. "Where are the other residents now?"

"Everyone else is already working on their projects. Everyone else got here on time."

The windows in my work space had screens between them and the glass. In that space there were several trapped hornets. They were moving around very slowly. Every once in a while, they would buzz into the glass, trying to escape.

I didn't know if the other residents had the same problem with insects. All the other doors were closed when I came in.

When I opened my laptop, I had an e-mail from my husband. It said: "According to this article, the key to a successful colony experience is getting into a routine. Try to set daily goals for yourself, so that you can complete your project in the alloted residency time."

I'd been struggling on a project for some time, or at least I liked to say I was struggling on it. Mostly I worked on it only a few minutes or maybe an hour each week. That way, I could at least tell other people that I was working on the project and not be entirely untruthful.

Since I was now at the colony, I felt a great deal of pressure to be truly working on it, working on it to the point of struggling. To facilitate the struggle, I took my husband's advice and set goals for myself. A certain percentage of the project completed per day.

Because the building was a barn, the sides of one wall sloped over my head. The walls were all white, and the way the light was reflected through the room made me feel as if the curved wall was going to collapse on me. I told myself that the wall was my project, and that if I didn't push it up straight soon, I would be crushed.

Although the colony only accepted a few residents at a time, both barns were very large. It was easy to work and not see the other residents. Mostly I heard them at night. When I was lying in bed and trying to read, they would be talking softly and the walls would muffle their voices into unintelligible words. Their voices sounded like wind breezing through wet leaves.

Sometimes, when I was pacing around my studio by a window, I would see a pale form out of the corner of my eye moving down the path between the two barns. By the time I paced back, they would be gone.

The only residents I saw up close were the insects. In addition to the hornets flying into the windows, there were a large number of furry caterpillars crawling on the first floor of the sleeping barn. I saw them squirming in and out of the doors of the other residents. I couldn't remember if they were the poisonous kind or even if caterpillars were ever poisonous. If I woke up in the middle of the night, I made sure to shine a flashlight on the floor as I walked.

There was a schedule of the moon printed on the wall of the first barn. It showed when the full moon was coming, and someone had circled the moon with a red marker and written "gathering!" under it.

I figured the gathering would be at the field where the famous artist had thrown parties. I marked the day on my own calendar.

My work on the project was going slower than I had counted on. I was unsure if I was struggling or merely struggling to struggle. Every time I sat down to work, a great fatigue came over me. It was as if the project was attempting to drain my life force. Each hour of struggle was causing me to fade away a little more.

Yet I told myself that a gathering with the other members of the colony might stimulate me in the necessary ways.

When the full moon came, I took out a scarf and a flashlight and looked for the other residents' lights swaying on the path. I didn't see any, and when I stepped outside I felt foolish. The moon was so bright there was no need for flashlights. I slid mine into my pocket and headed to the field.

Everything was tinted blue. It was like walking through deep ocean water. I even had the sensation I was drowning as the leaves swirled around my feet. Perhaps it was a result of anxiety over my work, or rather lack of work, on the project.

When I got down to the bottom of the path, there was a large, square field. The field had not been in use for some time and was covered in waist-high grass. On the far side of the field, a few hundred feet away, was the rest of the forest. Somehow, the way the moon was shining made it look as if the forest was two-dimensional. The black outlines of trees were pasted like construction paper against the dark blue sky.

I didn't see any of the other residents, but then there hadn't been a specified time.

I lay down on the short grass at the edge of the overgrown field. The sky was even bluer, and the small stars seemed to be sinking away from me.

Watching the dwindling points of light, I started to think, again, about my project. I believe I started the project around the time I met my soon-to-be ex-husband, although he was, of course, not even my husband at that time. I had been working on the project for so long that the beginning was as hard to make out as the end.

My anxiety about the project was overcoming the peacefulness of the night sky. I stood up and brushed off the dirt, hoping no ticks had crawled on me. I could hear a faint noise, like cans rattling in the distance. Then I noticed that on top of the flattened trees sat a group of pale figures. Their faces were smooth and thin, like old bars of soap. They were allowing their elongated limbs to blow in the breeze. Against the black trees and blue skies, it looked almost as if they were emitting light. I wondered how long they had been there, watching me.

Their legs were hanging over the trees in a way that should be impossible unless the trees were only two-dimensional. A few of them got up and walked around. Perhaps it was the distance, but it looked as if their features had faded way.

They seemed to be gesturing for me to come toward them. They were making long, swooping motions with their arms and hands, or what I took for hands. It seemed their arms ended in flat paddles with no discernible fingers.

I wanted to go across to them, to be part of the group.

When I turned on my flashlight to find a path through the high grass, they scattered and fell back behind the tree line where I couldn't see them.

"Wait," I said, but only loudly enough for myself to hear.

I started to walk through the field. There were thorny bushes hiding in the grass that cut at my clothes. I couldn't see the figures anymore. I stopped and turned back.

All of the doors in the barn were open when I went to bed.

The next day I moved my desk to the window. The hornets had died and collected at the bottom of the screen in a clump. I opened the screen and dumped their bodies into a coffee mug.

I tried to work on the project and watch at the same time. I thought I saw one of the tall, pale figures sprint along the path in a blur between the two barns.

When the sun set, I got my flashlight and scarf and went down to the field again. If the figures had been there the one night, it stood to reason they might be there another.

Although the moon was still engorged, there were dark clouds rolling across the sky. I had to use my flashlight most of the way down. I tried turning it off before I got to the field, but the pale figures had seen it and climbed down behind the trees before I could call them.

My husband e-mailed me and asked if I was "settling into the necessary routine." Those were his words: "settle" and "necessary." I wrote back that I had settled on a routine, which was true.

Each day, I was hitting my daily goal on the project, but each day it seemed that the scope of the project elongated. Each finished part necessitated two new parts, to be completed down the line. I kept reaching what I thought would be the end of the project, which now was merely another middle point. These middles stretched endlessly.

I tried knocking on the doors, politely of course. The other residents never answered. When I pressed my ear to their doors, I thought I could make out the sounds of people trying to hold their breath.

Going down to the field became part of my routine. There was never anybody else there, but I sat in the grass and listened to the distant noises that I took to be coyotes and owls. The moon was not nearly as bright anymore, and everything was in shades of gray.

One night, after a particularly draining day of work on the project, I kicked off my shoes. I dropped my jacket and shirt and pants on the ground. Naked, I was as pale as they had been in the dark. I thought if they were gathering somewhere in the trees, maybe their eyes were better than mine and would spot me and think of me as one of their own.

I waded into the tall grass.

The next day, my work routine was interrupted by the colony phone. The phone had not rung the entire time I was there. I waited with my ear pressed against the door, hoping I'd catch someone answering. On the tenth ring, I went into the hall.

"Hello?" I said.

"Good. It's you. I was hoping you'd be the one to answer." The voice sounded exactly like my husband's, but soon I realized it was actually the director of the colony.

The director said that she was very sorry, but that she was going to have to ask me to leave. There had been, in her words, "many complaints" about my "disruptive behavior" at the colony.

I started to apologize, saying that I hadn't tried to disrupt anything. The director of the colony sighed. She said she was sorry, and that this never, or at any rate almost never, happened. Yet her hands were tied.

"I hope you got some work in, for your sake," she said.

"But my project," I said. "I'm only just getting into a routine."

"I can give you a few hours," the director said, "to get your things in order."

A few hours later, a taxi appeared on the colony driveway.

I got inside.

ROUTINE

This morning I murder your mother, but then I always murder your mother. You're in the barricaded bathroom weeping or possibly asleep. I use the machete as quietly as I can.

I understand why you can't kill your mother, but if I'm being honest, it's hard on me too. Even with strips of skin hanging off her flesh like peeling paint, she bears an uncanny resemblance to you. You've always had her proud cheeks and slightly sunken eyes.

Your mother dies slowly, moaning all the way down. This is the worst part. I would never admit this to you, but your mother's moans recall the moans you made when we used to make love. Although we no longer have the strength to couple anymore, it is when I murder your mother that those happy memories come back to me.

One of your mother's lopped-off hands falls on my boot. I pick up the hand and begin moving her, piece by piece, to the front yard. I move a safe distance away and collapse on the ground.

But your mother returns earlier than normal this time. Her parts recollecting, her long-dead flesh willing itself to still more life.

I roll over and pull the machete from her femur. It has dulled on her bones. This time it takes twice the effort, twice the strokes, and this when your mother is only half-reformed.

It was easier to murder your mother when we had the bullets, and easier still when we had the shotgun shells. Then again, what part of life isn't harder these days?

This time, I find the shovel and begin to dig a pit. My fingers blister on the wooden handle. My legs ache.

I push the parts of your murdered mother into the pit one by one.

I get the gasoline that we foraged from the neighbors' charred car. It spills on my hands, burning the blisters. I'm too weak to even cry.

I shuffle back to the house, the smoke of your mother in my clothes.

Do you remember when we first came to this house? It was the first home either of us had ever owned. Our own little cottage in the woods, with a big red mailbox and a hammock out back. We thought we had our whole lives ahead of us.

I want to say it was a happier time then, but they weren't all happy times. We fought incessantly, and our income dried up along with the creek out back. You were still very beautiful to me, yet cold. I was afraid to wake you when I came home at night.

There was happiness too. There were days we lay in bed together until sundown, covered in sweat. Yet the bad times seemed destined to keep coming back, the same way your mother must reform and be murdered each day.

I find you in the bedroom. The sun is going down, and in the dying light, your skin looks almost as blue as your mother's. How long have you been lying there, still?

Tomorrow, when the remains of your mother dust off their ashes and return, I will have to murder her again. The only way to break this cycle is by failing. If I fail, then you will have to murder me alongside your mother, or else I will have to murder you alongside her, or perhaps, if we are lucky, some other people huddled in some other house will have to murder the three of us together.

A nne gave Arthur a cold look when he opened the door. He was in coattails and balancing a tray of iced drinks with a gloved hand.

"Arthur, you didn't tell us this was a costume party!" Roberta said.

This was just like Arthur, Anne thought. Always doing something nasty and telling you when it was too late.

Then another Arthur walked out of the kitchen wearing a smile and a blue windowpane suit. "I see you've met my butler," the new Arthur said. He stood next to the first Arthur and let out a laugh.

Anne's eyes got very large, and her mouth opened a little bit. Roberta reached out and squeezed the first Arthur's cheek with her thumb and forefinger.

"It feels so lifelike," she said with delight. "What is it? Latex?"

"Roberta, you're such a spark plug," Arthur in the blue suit said, giving her a kiss on the cheek. "And, Anne, you look like one in a million."

A few weeks ago, Arthur had gone inside part of Anne. Soon after that, Arthur had gone inside several parts of Roberta. Roberta and Anne were old friends. The issue was still unresolved.

Arthur was an architect and owned the entire floor. Large glass walls exposed the twinkling darkness of the city. The interior was divided into new geometry by bright wood walls and paper doors. In the largest room, a half-dozen guests were sipping cocktails and admiring a marble sculpture of Athena budding out of the head of Zeus.

"Well, spill the beans. How is it made?" Roberta demanded.

Arthur in the blue suit put his arm around Arthur in the butler outfit. "Please, Roberta. He isn't a *how*, he's a *who*."

"I need to use the bathroom," Roberta said angrily. "Don't explain anything until I get back."

Anne and the Arthurs looked at each other. The two men's faces were identical but showed very different expressions. One of them was smiling politely.

"The whole ordeal was really very painless," Arthur was saying to the multiplying crowd. "They run a few tests, checking the genes for quality I suppose, and then prick out a thimbleful of blood when you aren't looking. You come back to the laboratory six months later, and your custom-made man—or woman, as the case may be—is complete."

"Talk about bespoke!" someone said.

"It cost a pretty penny, I can tell you that," Arthur said. "But simply everybody who is anybody is going to have one soon."

"Arthur, you devil!" Roberta said with a squeal.

Anne had only been at the party one hour and was already feeling drained. Her necklace was heavy, plus they didn't even have cocktail onions for her martini. The problem with parties is that you could never relax and be yourself. Anne wished she were floating in a hot bath instead of trying to avoid Arthur in a noisy crowd. Two of him at that!

Anne's olive bobbed around her glass as Roberta scraped some caviar onto her cracker. She noticed that Roberta looked taller than her, thanks to three-inch heels. Why had Anne worn flats? She bet Roberta would surgically implant robotic heel extensions, if she only could afford it.

There was a thunderstorm brewing outside, which brightened the party with strobic flashes. A new guest materialized every ten minutes or so.

Anne wandered from the main group. She said hello to the Hoffmanns, the wife of whom was a psychologist who had once declared, at another awful party, that Anne's love of salty foods was a clear expression of sexual exasperation.

"What does this mean for Rank's theory of the double?" the husband was saying.

Suddenly an Arthur appeared beside her. It was the cloned Arthur in the butler suit.

"Whoops, I didn't see you there," Anne said.

This Arthur gave her a thin smile. He took her empty glass and arranged it next to another on his tray. The thunder clapped its clap outside.

"Cold weather today," Anne offered.

"I haven't been outside." He looked at Anne with an expression she didn't even know Arthur's face was capable of making. "He hasn't let me outside since the cloning."

"That's awful," Anne said. "Isn't that exactly like Arthur? The brute!"

The Arthur in the butler suit took a step back. He looked surprisingly hurt. "I'm Arthur too, you know."

The original Arthur and Anne were alone in the library. He was holding his face very close to hers. She could smell the Scotch tiptoeing on his breath. Anne's back was pressed against the spines.

"But what about Roberta?" Anne said.

Arthur fingered the strap of her dress. He touched his forehead lightly to hers.

"Right now, there's only you and me. The only two people in the world."

Arthur brought his teeth down gently on Anne's lower lip. She closed her eyes and pushed against him. This is how it had been in the beginning, the two of them hidden, alone, and groping.

Anne opened her eyes and saw the other Arthur standing in the doorway. His eyes were tight with anger, and he had something dark and heavy in his hands. Then there was a loud clap of thunder.

"Oh!" Anne said.

Arthur pulled away. His face was startled. He slowly turned around. "Ah, right, the toast," he said, reaching for the bottle of champagne. "Is it already ten? You'll have to excuse me."

The two Arthurs walked back to the main room. Anne tried to decide if she wanted to follow.

Roberta had her dress hiked up around her waist. Her stream hissed into Arthur's large toilet. Her skin looked very tan pressed against the porcelain.

"You just had to get at him. You're insatiable! The party isn't even half over yet."

Roberta ripped off some toilet paper and folded it neatly three times.

"I'm not going to say sorry, and anyway, he came on to me."

"Ho ho!" Roberta said. "All's fair in love and war, is that it?" She clicked out of the bathroom on her heels.

Anne stayed, looking at her tired face in the mirror for a bit.

The party was teeming now. Anne's shoulders bounced back and forth as she tried to get a drink.

She thought she saw Arthur and Roberta head off for one of

the back rooms. "Well doesn't that just beat all," she whispered to herself.

Anne finished the rest of her drink and placed it on the stereo speaker. It was the third martini glass she had placed on the stereo speaker. She thought it was about time to tell Arthur and Roberta a thing or two in a loud voice.

She moved her way through the crowd saying "hello" and "excuse me" to the people she knew. As she moved through the hallway, someone grabbed her elbow and yanked her into the study.

"I've been waiting to get you alone."

"Help!" Anne yelled, trying to break his grip. "This mutant is attacking me."

"I'm not attacking you," the Arthur in the butler suit said. "And I'm not a mutant."

The party was very loud outside, and no one came to rattle the door.

"Then what do you want?"

He shushed her with his finger, even though she was using a normal volume. He leaned in close, holding her forearm with his white glove.

"I have a horrible secret to tell you," he whispered. He paused, his heavy breath heating Anne's left ear. "*I'm Arthur.*"

"Yes, yes," she said, waving her hand. "Arthur explained the whole process. You are him, he is you, yada yada."

Anne realized they were in the coatroom. There was a large, furry hump of them on the table. Finally, she could just grab her things and go.

"No, I'm the *real* Arthur. The other one is the clone and masquerading as me."

This was all getting to be too much for Anne. She sat down in a leather wing chair and crossed her legs.

The Arthur in the butler suit knelt down beside her. He made his voice low and grave.

"Something must have gone wrong in the lab. He looks just like me, but he isn't the same. He overpowered me when I took him home and locked me in the closet, feeding me nothing except scones and tonic water for days."

Anne felt goose bumps rise along her arms.

"There is an evil in him." Arthur's eyes started to tear up. He rubbed them with his knuckles. "I suppose it's in me too. I was nasty to my brother and used to throw rocks at small animals as a child. I've struggled my whole life to contain it."

Anne put a comforting hand on his shoulder. She didn't know what else to do.

"I should never have paid those doctors to play God. What have I unleashed on the world?"

Arthur was weeping into one hand. With his other, Arthur slid a thin vial of green liquid from his inside coat pocket and slipped it into Anne's hand.

"Anne, you know I love you. I would never hurt you. That wasn't me who slept with Roberta, it was the clone! He only threw this party to torture me." Arthur was still holding her hand. He rubbed his thumb around her palm.

"Why am I supposed to believe you?" she said. Her breath was short, and she gripped the arms of the chair. She looked at the vial of green liquid in her free hand. There was a small skull and crossbones sticker affixed to it.

"You must decide for yourself," he said, hanging his head. "But his genes are unstable. He is growing more powerful and erratic every minute."

"What does this have to do with me?" Anne said.

"You're the only one who can get close enough to him. He trusts you. Because I trust you."

• • •

Anne decided she didn't care who was the real Arthur and who was the fake. What if the cloning process had made the new Arthur possess a higher concentration of essential Arthurness? Could he be even more Arthur than Arthur? And in that case, how could you say which Arthur was real? It wasn't a question she was ready to handle.

And yet, despite everything, she didn't want Roberta to get hurt.

"I've always said it's the clothes that make the man," Arthur was saying to Roberta as Anne walked into the room. She was walking slowly, but her heart was beating very fast.

Arthur had Roberta's hand in his, and he slid one of her fingers into his mouth and bit down.

"Ouch!" Roberta said with a giggle. Her finger was bleeding a little bit. "You scoundrel."

When Arthur saw Anne, his eyes narrowed. "Where have you been?" he demanded.

Anne waved one hand toward another part of the apartment. In the other, she hid the vial in a fist. "I need to talk to Roberta," she said.

Anne and Arthur exchanged looks and laughed together, but Roberta came anyway. Anne took Roberta out onto the balcony and slid the glass door shut.

"Did you see Jerome and Chiara Dopp?" Roberta said. "I told you that simply everybody who's anybody would be here. Aren't you glad we came?"

Roberta's words were slurred, and her eyes seemed to be swimming around in her skull. Anne's head was swimming too.

"Listen, have you noticed anything strange about Arthur? He doesn't seem quite like his usual self, right?"

Roberta groaned.

"Can't we talk about something else? Arthur is a free man. He can do whatever he wants."

"But doesn't he seem more, I don't know, *aggressive?*"

"That's it," Roberta said, "I'm getting another drink."

Anne could see the Arthur in the butler suit looking at her from across the room. His eyes were pleading, and he was making frantic gestures. The other Arthur had his arms around both Roberta and Anne now.

Why was this Anne's decision to make? She was drunk and tired and sick of everyone and everything. She just wanted to go home and sleep a peaceful sleep in her own bed.

"If only I could keep both of you here for myself!" Arthur in the blue suit said.

Anne pretended to laugh. Roberta was laughing too, but shot Anne a nasty look.

"Maybe Anne can go freshen your drink," Roberta offered. "So we can talk *alone.*"

Anne took the empty glass and huffed off to the bar.

Arthur's body twitched on the Oriental rug for quite some time.

It was late in the night, and the few remaining guests were standing aghast around the foyer. Anne was starting to sober up.

"Oh god. Oh god," she muttered. The empty vial slipped out of her hand and clinked on the tiles. How would she know if she killed the right one?

Roberta came bolting in from the kitchen.

"If you couldn't have him, nobody could. Is that it? You've never been happy for me, not once in my whole life!" Roberta started to cry. "There were two of them. We could have worked something out."

The remaining Arthur knelt down beside the body and solemnly slid down the eyelids.

He stood up and looked at Anne. Roberta stared at Anne and pulled out her cell phone, threatening to call the police. The thunder rumbled softly in the distance. The three of them stood over the body, the seconds doubling and doubling as they tried to anticipate what would happen next.

MEGAFAUNA

WHAT WE HAVE SURMISED ABOUT
THE JOHN ADAMS INCARNATION

Although much remains unclear about John Adams (alternatively referred to in recovered documents as Jon Adam, John Adems, and the Adams Abomination), recent drone expeditions into the Charred Continent have unearthed new artifacts that lead us closer to understanding this mysterious entity.

Long assumed to be a prince or demon of a lesser cult, we now know that John Adams was an important figure in the dominant United Statsian mythology. He appears to have originally been conceived as a familiar or minion of George Washington, the first of the hundred tyrants that are said to have ruled the country until its infamous, self-inflicted demise. It was only later that John Adams was celebrated as a deity in his own right. His physical manifestation is a source of debate. Certain scholars suggest he was worshipped as an enormous, goat-like god or perhaps a sentient birch tree—referred to as the Braintree—by the Cults of Puritan that populated the region now known as the Twice-Damned Seaboard. Often he is portrayed as a fat, sullen man, whose lips seem curled in a perpetual frown.

As the second of the early tyrants—likely monarchs who were worshipped as divine, although possibly purely mythological figures—John Adams can be placed squarely in what may be called the "Constitutional Pantheon" of the United Statsian religion. His chief rivals in this group were Alexander "the Uncrowned" Hamilton and Thomas Jefferson, the latter of whom would usurp his throne. It is believed that Adams's symbols were the split acorn, the horned hair, and the first feather of the newborn eagle.

The acolytes of Adams do not appear to have had as much influence as the followers of more prominent gods, such as Benjamin Franklin, Lincoln of the Logs, or the Great Traitor Burr (a title that was perhaps ironic given his apparent influence among the Southern lands). Of all the sacred coins and wood pulp currency sheets that have been unearthed from the burnt rubble, none have featured the visage of John Adams—a fact that is rather unusual among the early tyrants.

Here it must be noted that many scholars now believe these beings were not necessarily viewed as *separate* by the United Statsians, but rather different *incarnations* of the one "founding father" deity, also known as George Washington—the first incarnation—Uncle Sam, or the First and the Last, the Truth and the Lie. The Founding Father, in this conception, was a shape-shifting and eternal god believed to have formed the nation by tearing apart fragments of the gigantic Life Tree with his "teeth of wood" and regurgitating fifty large bark chunks into the sea to form the collected states.

In his fleeting incarnation as John Adams, the Founding Father was pale, bloated, and quick to anger. His commandments were enforced by a set of terrifying minions known only as the Midnight Judges. Scholars agree that this was a tumultuous time for early United Statsian society, as the wars with rival nations such as Imperial France and Britain of the First Decay had taken their tolls on the populace. The newly formed United States was working to define itself and struggling with enemies both within and without. The monstrous John Adams incarnation likely provided a feeling of strength and destiny to the huddled and starving United Statsians.

Although harsh in demeanor and despised among the citizenry, the John Adams incarnation is given credit for defeating the rival gods of Imperial France—almost certainly symbolic of an actual conflict known mysteriously as the Quasi War—in a grand battle that raged "atop the purple mountains and shining seas" for twelve cycles before John Adams emerged bloodied and tired, yet victorious.

With the enemies defeated and peace at hand, the need for the brutal John Adams incarnation had passed. He had served his people and maintained the power of the new nation. When he looked on what he had wrought, John Adams is said to have let out a month-long howl from the center of the sacred House in White—a scream so terrible in force it rendered an entire generation deaf and ripped apart the very earth, forming the great canyon of the western desert, a fissure the Adams incarnation disappeared into only to reemerge weeks later as the kindly Jefferson form.

Hopefully continued archeological expeditions into the continent will uncover more findings to expand our understanding of the ancient United Statsian religion and society. It is important to remember that the early United Statsians were a frightened, but proud, people. Despite the lower levels of spectrum radiation and thinner dust-metal storms, the world was as confusing and painful a place to them as it is to us now. Although their religion may strike us as arcane and barbaric, you must put yourself in their mindset. They were building a new society in a strange and foreign land. The night was dark; the beasts were loud. Death, in all its myriad incarnations, was, as always, right around the corner.

DARK AIR

How we ended up in those backwoods hills was Iris said we needed to "get a little air," and Dolan added, "country air!" and that was that. Iris was my lover, and Dolan was her roommate I'd never liked. All of us were alive, at that point.

I had no problem with city air. I figured it was the same air out there as in here, but the decision had been made in my presence without my participation.

"You know what we mean, goofus," Dolan said. "The noise. The lights."

Iris giggled and put her hand on Dolan's arm. They had their own private definition of humor.

A few hours later we were rolling through the hills. We'd been in the car the whole time, and we had the windows up, AC blasting. We hadn't yet felt the country air.

The roads in these mountains were littered with signs. Caution for this, danger about that. Falling rocks, bobcat crossing, dangerous incline. There must have been a dozen ways for us to be crushed or torn apart.

"You never see green like this in the city," Iris was saying. She clicked away with her phone as we rounded a chunk of mountain that had been blown open with dynamite.

"You live by the park," I said. "The park is green."

"That's a fake green. I mean *real* green."

"This is the green," Dolan said, "that's good for the soul."

Dolan was giving out the directions, steering us toward one of the "Top 10 Secluded Spots for Selfies" he'd read about online. There was a basket of turkey sandwiches and seltzer water in the back.

Dolan wasn't wearing his seat belt, and as I drove I imagined the door popping open when we went around a sharp turn, then watching him tumble down the cliff and disappear.

After that, maybe Iris and I could get a fresh start on our own.

The dinky towns and small shops had died out miles before, and we still hadn't found Dolan's spot. Even the danger signs were worn away here, rusted or obscured with splatters of brown goo. The trees were a sickly yellow-green. I rolled down my window, but there was a bad smell in the air.

Iris and Dolan were in the back talking about books I'd never read.

"It's bad air up here," I said. "Something huge must have died, like a bigfoot."

"You're so negative all the time," Iris said. She reached up to plug in her phone's playlist.

"Yeah, lighten up and soak in this country sun," Dolan chimed in.

I shut up and let the landscape roll past me. I had a lot of things to think about anyway, from where things were going with Iris to what the hell I was even doing with my life. I was at that age where it seemed as if everything was still possible but only to someone else. I lived in the city in a small apartment I hated and crashed most nights with a girlfriend who sometimes wasn't even there.

At the top of one hill, I saw a white goat standing on a rock. Its horned head twisted to follow our car as we passed.

He had some wound in the middle of his forehead that looked like a misplaced eye.

"Maybe it's time to head back," I said, but no one responded. Dolan had his headphones on, and Iris was pretending to sleep.

"Hey, I said—"

I think that's around when the creature burst from the bushes on the side of the road. It was black and pink and skittered across the pavement without using its wings. When we hit it, the left front tire popped, and we started fishtailing. Dolan and Iris were both awake now and screaming.

I swung the wheel to the right and allowed the rock face to stop us. The car filled with dust, and my face was smashed into the dense pillow of an air bag. The screams were muffled now. Slowly the air bags deflated, and we wiped the blood from our bruised noses with our sleeves.

"What the hell did you do that for?" Iris shouted.

"My car! My fucking car!" Dolan moaned in a continuous loop.

Sitting there, shirt stained with blood, Iris photographing her face "for the records," I had the feeling that things between us might be reaching the end.

When we went over to look at the creature, it was mostly flattened. It looked like a crow, except the feathers had fallen off its back. Underneath, the flesh was scaly and pink. The exposed skin was split in half by a row of translucent spikes. The spikes were moving slightly, pointing first in this direction then in that. The smell made me wrinkle my nose. It was an oddly sweet smell to find outdoors, like an open vat of lollipop flavoring.

For some reason, bumblebees were hovering above the carcass like buzzards. They made me dizzy. Iris started dry heaving.

"Bees!" Dolan shrieked. He grabbed Iris and held her in front of him. "First my car, now killer bees."

"Let's get out of here," Iris said. She sounded defeated. "Let's just go home."

"Okay," I said, but I wanted to get a closer look and maybe a few photos of this thing. I figured they might get me some favorites and likes on the internet.

When I squatted close, I noticed that alongside the undulating spikes there were two watery ovals ringed with a ridge of veined flesh. They looked like eyeballs without the pupils. I wanted to reach out a finger and poke one.

When I did, the creature came back to life.

After things calmed down, I saw Dolan on his back in the road. I had closed my eyes and run away, swatting bees blindly with my hands. One of them had stung me on the neck. Dolan was doing much worse, though. His whole face was like an over-inflated balloon. His skin was turning a dark, bruised red. Foam pooled beside his cheek on the pavement.

"Oh my god," Iris said. "We have to get him to a hospital."

I'd always suspected she was cheating on me with Dolan. This didn't seem like the time to be thinking about that, but watching her kneel to cradle his head, I couldn't help it.

"There aren't any hospitals around here. I haven't seen a town for miles."

"We have to do something!"

Her phone wasn't getting any signal, and mine was dead. I looked around and tried to think. A little way down the road there was an old dirt path leading into the woods. It looked sparsely used, but at the foot there was a bashed-in mailbox labeled "The Scintleys."

"There's a driveway over there," I pointed.

The creature had made it another fifty feet but was lying still again. The bees descended on it in a swarm. The noise was thunderous.

We got Dolan up on his feet and put his arms around our shoulders. He was looking a little better and even gurgled some words that sounded like either "a plan" or "the pain!" The front of his shirt was stained with drool.

It took us a little while to get in sight of the house. Dolan was still breathing, but Iris and I were doing all the work. There were porch lights on at one point, and I noted it to Iris, but when I looked back they had been turned out. There was a string of faded prayer flags hanging on the porch. In the yard, a metal sculpture covered in glass bottles clinked in the wind.

We heard shuffling behind the door when we buzzed the buzzer.

"Hey! Hey!" Iris said and kept pressing the button. I was stooped under the weight of Dolan.

It was starting to get late. The sky was draining of color, and I could no longer see the sun through the patchwork of trees. I scratched the back of my neck where the bee had stung me and felt the hard, swelling bump.

Iris kept banging away.

Finally, a man and a woman opened the door. They were both wearing scarves around their necks, gloves, and long-sleeve tie-dyed shirts. I myself was sweating puddles in a shirt and jeans. I was worried they were from one of those weird religions that thought flesh was an abomination.

The bundled couple surveyed us for a few seconds. "You with the government?" the man said when he'd worked up to our faces. His beard was overgrown, and there were little pink crumbs dotting his red lips.

"Well, he works for the Department of Education," I said, pointing a thumb at Dolan.

Iris gave me a look that made me shut up quick. "What?"

she said. "No, we aren't with the government. We got in an accident down the road because some bird ran in front of us, or flew or something, and my friend got stung by bees, and he can't get stung by bees because it makes him swell up and not breathe, and we need to use a phone to get him to a hospital quick, please!"

"We don't have a phone up here," the man said slowly. "We try to live in harmony with our surroundings." Other than the clothes that covered most of their flesh, the two of them looked healthy and vital. When they smiled, I could see all of their teeth.

Soon a small girl, also covered up to her chin, appeared between their legs. "Can they stay for dinner?" the child said.

"George," the woman said tenderly. "Invite them in. We're still all children of the same cosmos, aren't we?"

The woman guided us to a couch to rest Dolan on. His chest was rising and falling rhythmically now. His face was still grotesque, but it seemed he'd live.

"I'll make some herbal tea that will soothe his throat," the woman said. She told us her name was Feather and shook a pair of feathers stuck in her braid. "Like these," she said.

"Tell me again what this crow looked like," George said. He tied his own long hair back in a ponytail. "Don't spare any details."

After we went over it again, he said he'd go take a look at our car and headed out.

When they'd both left, I leaned over and rubbed Iris's back. The sun was fading and letting in warm, pink light.

"It's kind of romantic up here, isn't it?" I whispered.

Iris was wiping drool off Dolan's chin. "What the fuck is wrong with you?" she said.

I don't know why I'd said it. I think I was just trying to lighten

DARK AIR

the mood, because I was starting to get weirded out about the place. The last light of the day had slithered away, and the woman in the kitchen was knocking pots together. I kept thinking about the three-eyed goat and roadkill crow.

"Maybe we shouldn't drink anything," I said. "There might be something in the water up here."

"What do you know about water purity?" she said.

"I'm just saying I don't know about these people. They're wrapped up like mummies in the middle of summer."

"Now you're a fashion expert too?" Iris hissed.

Lately, Iris and I were always talking like this. We'd been good in the beginning, but along the way things had fallen off the rails. Maybe it was her fault, and maybe it was mine. More likely it was Dolan's, but either way we were fighting more, and I was waking up every morning cold and angry.

The day drained away with Iris and Dolan on one couch and me stewing in my private stew. In that way, it was becoming too much like every other day.

Iris said it wasn't polite to walk around without permission, but sitting still was making me paranoid. Maybe it was the stale air in that room or the finger paintings of wildlife on the walls. Iris was rubbing Dolan's chest and telling him it would be okay. I kept thinking about Dolan and Iris naked and undulating against each other's pink flesh. The beesting on my neck was still swelling, and it hurt to touch. I took a few sips of Feather's tepid, salmon-colored tea.

At some point, I nodded off.

In my dream, I was in a field of corn. The corn immediately around me had been flattened into a crop circle by asshole teenagers. The stalks around the circle were taller than me and bright green. They were so fresh they were dripping with perspiration.

The old goat with the eye in the middle of its head walked out of the corn and into the circle. The crow was riding on its head between the horns. It flopped off the goat's head and scurried across the downed corn toward me, pulling itself forward with its wings. It began cawing and crawling up my leg. Then it expired and fell to the ground.

The goat let out a tortured howl, and I looked back up. It stared at me with all three eyes. A seam appeared above its nose, then stretched back across its head. When the seam made its way around to the chin, the goat's skin and dirty white fur fell off, half to the left and half to the right.

I was wrong about the crow. It had come back to life and was trying to scale my leg. I could feel its claws digging into my shin.

Underneath the goat's skin was a bloody mess that looked nothing like a goat. Then I realized it wasn't a goat, it was Dolan! He was naked and covered in blood. There were rows of spikes going down his arms and legs.

"What the hell is up with you and Iris?" I said.

In response, the Dolan-goat let out another tortured howl, and another seam appeared. I could see something black and rubbery inside. Before this new seam could fully open, I was awoken to another Dolan shouting. This Dolan had one hand gripping my arm and the other gripping Iris's.

"Ow!" she said, then, "You're awake, thank god."

I guess his throat was still swollen up, because he could barely talk. His words sounded like someone gargling with blood. "He's cutting the brake lines."

"Who?"

"He must destroy one vessel to trap another."

Feather was two rooms away. I saw her poke her head out the kitchen door and squint at us.

Iris's eyes were wild, but I was confused. "What are you even talking about, Dolan?"

"The bearded man," Dolan said, talking more quietly now and spitting up a bit of blood and foam.

"You mean George?" Iris said. "He's fixing the car. We're getting out of here and getting you to a hospital. You'll be all right, I promise. You're gonna be A-OK."

Dolan closed his again. He seemed to be falling back to sleep.

"No. I heard him tell the woman," he said.

"Dolan, he isn't even in the house."

"He talks without lips. They won't let us leave. The flesh in his brain won't allow it."

When George finally came back, Dolan was snoring. George stood in the doorway and shook his head.

"We can fix the tire, but the engine is busted. You'll have to walk down the mountain to Gunderburg in the morning. You should get reception down there and be able to call a tow truck, but it isn't safe till first light. We'll fix you up a place to sleep in the spare room."

"Can't we just use your computer and get a cab up here?" Iris said.

"We don't use the internet. We don't need the government spying on us through the wires," George said. "And anyway, we got everything we need right here in these beautiful woods."

He left, saying he had to wash his hands. He was still wearing gloves.

"Let's head out now, before he gets back," Iris whispered.

"We can't carry Dolan down a whole mountain."

"We're going to have to. We aren't leaving him with paranoid hillbillies."

"I think they're hippies, not hillbillies," I said.

She gave me a look that said I didn't have a choice, then walked to the kitchen. "We really appreciate your hospitality, but we couldn't impose. Do you have a flashlight we could borrow? We'll head into town. We aren't afraid of the night."

The husband and wife gazed at each other for a minute or two without moving. Then the husband nodded and the wife turned back.

"Stay for dinner, at least," George said. "I'll make an all-natural herb paste to put on your friend's stings, and you guys can go on your way with a belly full of organic food. No one can say the Scintleys don't keep a house of healing and peace."

When George went to go "gather some herbs and berries" for the paste, I made an excuse to go use the bathroom. My neck was killing me, and I wanted to see what was up without worrying Iris.

The bathroom window was covered with old boards, but as I urinated I noticed a crack. I put my eye close. George was walking toward a cage with a long black rod, like a cattle prod. The cage was covered with a ratty old tarp. George lifted a corner of the tarp and rattled the cage. His back was blocking what was inside. I saw him switch on the cattle prod.

Around that time, I started to feel a pain in my forehead. It was a pain that came from sound, a swelling hum. I stumbled, knocking over the soap.

Someone banged on the door. "You all right in there?"

My heart was beating quickly, but I decided to get out and pretend nothing had happened.

When I left, Feather closed the door behind me without going in.

. . .

The paste that we put on Dolan's face was purple and chunky. It didn't look as if it had any herbs in it. Still, Dolan's face started to deflate, and he let out a pleased sigh. I sneaked a little to rub on the gumball-sized sting on my neck.

"He looks peaceful," the little girl said. She'd been standing in the doorway, pulling at the arms of her rag doll. "I bet he's dreaming about the stars."

One weird thing about dinner was that none of the Scintleys touched the normal food. There was roasted wild rabbit, a bowl of green beans, and mashed potatoes. They passed the plates around a few times, and Feather even took a scoop of potatoes, but all they actually chewed were fleshy pink strips laid out on a sterling silver platter. They didn't pass that platter to us.

"So what kind of plant is that?" Iris said. "Bamboo?"

"Something like that," George said.

"Try some!" the little girl said.

"Oh, they wouldn't like it, Clover," the mother said coldly. She turned to us, "It's from a species that's only native to these hills. An acquired taste. And we don't have much of it to spare. I'm sure you understand."

The little girl frowned and crossed her arms. The strips on the plate looked sticky and sweet. They were sitting in a pool of muddy yellow sauce.

Iris and I exchanged a look. She went back to poking her food with her fork. It didn't look like she'd eaten much. I hadn't either. My head was bothering me. The swarming noise had returned and was drowning my thoughts. It felt like a bad gin hangover, and I bent forward in pain. Some kind of liquid trickled out of my ear.

Then suddenly the noise cleared, as if it had been sucked away by a vacuum cleaner.

Why are you lying? Clover said, only not exactly. She was looking at her mother, yet her lips weren't moving.

Honeypot, we don't know yet if the flesh of the star-fallen is for them.

The crow-bitten has the aura, George's voice said, *but the other two are likely just allergic to bees.*

All three family members were still. They weren't even moving their utensils, and I had the sudden feeling I was in a wax museum. The buzzing noise started up in my head again suddenly. I squeezed my eyes shut and concentrated until it stopped.

But I want friends. I want to play. It's boring up here alone!

You know I'm not violent, darling, George's voice said, *but if you don't listen to your mother, I'll have to pull out the respect belt.*

"Hey," I said, "let's all calm down."

I immediately realized my error.

The three family members silently turned their heads toward me. George and Feather had their mouths agape. Clover was smiling.

"What the hell are you talking about?" Iris said, annoyed.

The rest of us didn't talk though. We were waiting for someone to make the first move.

He has the star-fallen aura. He heard!

Pretend nothing happened. We have to make sure the host has enough time.

"Excuse me," George said, enunciating every syllable. "I think I hear nature calling, so to speak."

He stood up and carefully put his chair back. He stretched his arms and scratched his bearded neck. I could see him looking at me from the corner of his eye.

"I'm going to check on Dolan," Iris said. "Thanks for the dinner, it was very, uh, well-balanced." When she stood up, Feather grabbed her hand.

"You haven't had dessert," she said. "I make a completely organic berry pie."

"Hey, don't grab me," Iris said and yanked at Feather's gloved hand. When she did, the glove came off, and Feather and Iris both gasped.

"What the fuck did you do to your hand?"

Feather's hand alighted back on Iris's. It wasn't a normal hand. It was swollen and bright pink, with rows of tiny spikes running down the middle of four fingers. Only the pinky had remained unchanged. Her fingernails on the other four fingers had fallen off, but the skin underneath looked odd. Each finger ended in the same watery, pupil-less eye.

"Oh dearie," she said, pulling her hand back and covering it with a napkin. "I guess the cat's out of the bag now."

We managed to get the family room door locked and began propping up furniture. Even from behind the shut door, I could hear the parents shouting at each other in my mind. Clover was laughing. My head was swimming in sound and adrenaline, and I could only hear fragments. *Does the woman have it too? . . . Will he want to join the circle? . . . This is serious, Clover . . . signal with burnt skin . . .* and so on.

"Dolan, we have to go. Wake up!" Tears ran down her face.

I went over to her, and she grabbed my hand. Her grip was so tight her fingernails dug into my skin, and I started bleeding.

"What did they do to him? What the fuck is wrong with these people?"

Dolan, if he was still Dolan, was lying engorged on the couch. His skin had turned even darker. It looked as if his entire body was one huge bruise. His stomach cavity was swelling outward, spilling over his jeans and remaining rib cage. You could see that several off the ribs had cracked where bits of bone had ripped through his shirt. Rivulets of pus dripped from little holes in his skin where tiny translucent bulbs had emerged. His eyes were closed and crusted with dark gunk.

Iris kept yelling "no" and pinching her face as if she was trying to wake up from a dream. I'd never been a big fan of Dolan, but even I didn't like seeing him like this. I wished we could all be back in that car, driving through the woods in our angry silence back to the city.

The Scintleys were knocking politely on the door. "Brother, sister, open the door and commune with us. You don't know the joy your friend has in store!"

"We need to get out of here," I said, trying to pull Iris up.

"Fuck you," Iris said quietly. She was weeping. "Do you even know what Dolan did for me? I had a life before we dated, you know. And it was a shitty life until Dolan helped me out. I'm not leaving him to die on a couch."

"We'll get help. We'll go get help and come back and save him."

She was trying to lift Dolan and wouldn't move. I tried to help her, and we got him almost standing. His skin was covered in sweat and goo. He slipped out of our arms and onto the rug. He let out a deep inhuman groan as he fell.

Iris balled her hands into fists and snarled, "Oh, we're coming back all right. We're coming back to fuck those fuckers up."

There was a side door that opened to the backyard. Iris and I sprinted toward the shack, holding hands. My heart was pulsing like a strobe light.

It was pretty dark out, and we ducked into the space between the shack and the covered cage to catch our breath. Iris leaned against the cage. "Those cocksuckers, those motherfuckers," she was saying between huffs.

I peeked over the edge of the cage and saw Feather in the light of the kitchen window. She was pointing out toward something behind their house with her deformed hand. It wasn't in our direction.

"We'll sneak down that slope and make our way back to the road," Iris said. "Then we'll come back with police and guns and fucking rapid dogs."

"Do you mean rabid dogs?"

"Both!"

"Sure," I said. "Okay. That's a plan." I was distracted though. My head was starting to buzz again, and the noise seemed to somehow be emanating from the cage. There was a presence in there cooing to me, like a mother to a child, without words. It wanted me to reach inside.

Iris slapped my hand. "What are you doing?" she whispered. "We need to go. We need to help Dolan."

The buzzing in my head made me close my eyes. I couldn't help it. It felt as if my insides were brittle, cracking glass. It was originating from the beesting on my neck. I reached back to rub it. When my fingertip touched the swollen sting on my neck, everything in front of me dissolved from black to white to black again.

I wasn't seeing Iris or any woods or house or tarp-covered cage. I was in a cyclopean pink cave at least as large as a football stadium. It was lit from undulating yellow orbs that sank from the ceilings, stretching out like drool from sleeping lips, until they snapped and splattered on the floor. When they splattered, their light disappeared. The cave itself was scaly, but pulsing. The floor surged and waned.

When I crawled forward, the scales of the floor opened up around my hands and feet. I sank in, and then the scales closed back. The toothless mouths of the floor gummed my elbows and knees. I could feel my skin being rubbed off. I cried out in pain.

There was a presence that was trying to speak to me, but it didn't know how. It was assaulting me, yelling things at me that weren't words or human feelings. I tried to say, "I don't understand," but when I did, a fissure opened between my bottom front teeth.

The fissure crept down my chest. I couldn't see it, but I could feel it splitting open down my stomach and all the way around. I could feel myself opening. I was sliding to each side. I tried to scream again, and my teeth fell out, replaced by small, stunted spikes that hurt my tongue. Then my eyes dripped away, running down my checks and hanging over the floor.

When they hit the cave floor, everything went black again.

Welcome back to this realm.

George was standing over me. He'd taken his scarf off, and I could see the swollen mound of spikes on his neck. He was holding a lantern with a bare, deformed hand. His other held the cattle prod at his side.

I looked around and didn't see Iris. Iris was always threatening to leave me, but I hadn't thought it would happen like this.

"I think we got off on the wrong foot," George said. "You can understand why we're wary of strangers. If the government found us, who knows what experiments their sick scientists would do. We have to protect it. We're all it has." *Plus you and me are brothers now, aren't we?*

"Brothers?"

"Let me show you something. Can you get on your feet?" He helped me up and motioned toward the cage. "Take a look and prepare to be amazed by what this universe contains," he said. His smile was gigantic. I couldn't tell if his teeth were real or covering something else.

I could feel that presence again, humming something to me. It was vibrating my spine. I didn't know what the hell it was trying to say. I pulled the tarp off the cage and immediately gasped and stepped backwards.

I don't know what kind of horror I was expecting, but my stomach was instantly filled with sadness.

The creature was about the size of a Great Dane and rested on its side on the bottom of the cage. It wasn't shaped quite like a dog though. The body was a distorted orb, wider at one end than the other. It looked almost like an elongated apple, except covered in cracked, pink flesh. Rows of translucent spikes ran down its body in five columns. They met up at a wrinkled sphincter at the top. The creature's body didn't move, but its spikes undulated up and down in a sad rhythm. Between the rows of spikes there were sets of large watery ovals that seemed to be eyes. A bit of yellow-green liquid, like pea soup, dripped out of one or two of them.

"Incredible, isn't it?" George said. "We found this wonder in the cornfield back there, flopping around on the ground like a fish yanked out of water." He held his hands together and bowed toward the cage.

"Where did it come from?"

"It fell here from another glorious world. We found a thick round rubber vessel nearby." He motioned off into the woods. "Its house, I guess. If you want proof of how mysterious the cosmos are, watch this."

George flicked on the cattle prod and jammed it inside.

The creature began convulsing, its spikes flailing in all directions. A sweet stench, like burnt garlic, surrounded us.

The message the creature was sending me was very clear now. Pain. Its hurt rained through my body, and by the scrunched-up look on George's face, his too. Then there was a thick ripping sound, like someone pulling apart an enormous steak with their hands.

"I can always feel its life force when I do that," he said.

When I looked back down, there were two creatures in the cage, identical in size and shape. They were both smaller than the one before.

"This creature doesn't even consume plants, much less animals. It sustains itself on electricity and makes love with it. It's how it reproduces. We've been eating its bounty, using every part like the Indians. We always keep one half of it alive and strong. If it wasn't for our care, it would have surely died already." George hung the lantern on a hook on the wall of the nearby shack. "It's been rewarding us too, transferring its aura to us and allowing our life forces to merge." *But you already know that, don't you?*

He pulled a small black pistol from the back of his pants. He used the gun to scratch the underside of his chin.

"I didn't eat any of it," I said.

"No, but I suppose those bees must have communed with it before stinging you. The crow put something different in your fellow traveler though. He isn't like you and me. Feather and I don't even know exactly what he will birth, but I think you can understand why we couldn't let you leave."

He pressed the side of the gun into his cheek, as if he was making a motion to fall asleep. "Well, I abhor guns, but I have to keep the forces in balance." He lowered the gun and fired. The new creature trembled once, and then was still.

The first creature's eyes turned dark. The spikes drooped downward, and a cloud of rank gas whiffed out of its wrinkly hole.

George scratched his beard with the barrel again. It must have still been hot, because I smelled a bit of singed hair. He smiled and put the gun back in his pants.

"Can't you feel how connected we are? I wasn't sure at first, but after you spoke at dinner I knew. This wonderful being has touched both of us and joined our chis."

He leaned his head back so he was facing the stars and let out a whoop.

I didn't even see Iris coming, but she whacked George pretty good in the back of the head. When he fell forward, his chin hit the cage, and his teeth smacked together with a wet crunch.

"You sick hippie hick!" She was on top of him now and gashing his back with a hatchet she'd found god knows where. His blood turned the dirt under him into mud. The mixture was dotted with broken bits of teeth. "You aren't nice people! You're sicko pervert assholes!"

Finally she stopped and stood over him, breathing rapidly. When she looked at me, I saw her face was splattered with blood. Some had gotten in her left eye, making her wink.

"Where did you learn to do that?" I said.

"It's not hard, you just swing," she said. "Are you okay?"

I said I thought I was and she smiled.

"Then let's get Dolan and get the hell back to the city."

"What about that thing? I don't want to leave it like that."

Iris looked in the cage and groaned.

"What kind of shit is that? A diseased walrus? I can't deal with this right now. I'm getting Dolan, and you're coming with me, and we're never coming out to this shit hole again."

Feather broke down in tears when she saw us walk by splattered in blood.

"Run, run to your room!" she said to Clover, shielding her with her body. She moaned George's name and started chanting in a language I didn't understand.

Iris walked right past her though, and I followed.

"Dolan," Iris said quietly. The thing she was talking to didn't look like Dolan to me. His flesh had sloughed off. His face was bunched up like a rubber mask on the floor.

In the cavity of Dolan, a thick black orb was expanding. It was half in, half out of Dolan. Bits of him clung to its curved sides. The stench of the room made me pinch my nose shut. A few dark strands extended out of the orb, writhing on the floor. Another strand had made its way out of Dolan's ear and slithered into the wall socket.

Iris was throbbing with tears. I pulled her away and hugged her. "Hey, it'll be all right. We're gonna be all right."

Iris pushed her hands up my chest in what I took to be a tender way. But when her hands reached my neck, she shoved me back violently.

"My fucking best friend is dead! It's not going to be all right, you dick! How did I ever even date you? What is wrong with your fucking brain?"

She tore at her hair and looked around the room with wild eyes. She ran a few feet toward one door, then turned and ran back toward the couch. She didn't seem to know what to do, but eventually she threw the axe at the orb. "This is bullshit!" she screamed.

I barely heard Feather yell, "It's not safe out of the cage, go back!" When I turned around, she was trying to shove the creature back out the door.

I'd left the cage door open before we came inside. I'd tried to project a message of peace and forgiveness.

The pink creature was moving toward the Dolan-orb, inching along like a worm. It stopped and turned to Feather. She was chanting her prayer and pushing with all her might. Then the top of the creature, where the rows of spikes converged on the sphincter, expanded open. The creature bunched up and, I guess, inhaled.

Feather's leg got sucked right in up to the knee. She screamed, hopping on her other leg. Her right leg was inside the creature for about three seconds, then the creature spat what was left back out. Fleshless bones hung from her kneecap. She tried to stand on both legs, but the bare bones collapsed with her weight, and she tumbled to the floor. She looked completely confused, and her eyes darted around. Blood poured over the white bones.

The creature did the same thing to her left leg. It sucked it in as she screamed, then spat it out as neat, white bones. The creature rolled a little to the left and regurgitated a pile of tendons, muscle, and blood. Feather was barely moving now. The creature shifted itself to face her twitching arm.

When Iris saw the creature continuing toward us, she shouted, "You aren't coming near Dolan, pus bag!"

I pulled her out of the way just as the thing was opening its hole. Iris struggled against me, but I held on.

Go on, we won't stop you, I tried to say to the creature. I concentrated as hard as I could. *I am sorry for what the man and woman did to you. We killed the bearded one for you.*

The creature's opening was facing us. I could see a strange yellow light inside. It stayed there for a few seconds, then clenched back up. It turned toward the black orb.

By this point, the orb had expanded to the size of the couch. The bottom was still expanding out of the cavity of Dolan. It didn't seem fully formed. A half-dozen thin threads were wrapped around the appliances in the room. You could hear the hum of the electricity moving through them.

The creature emitted a low rumble, and a part of the orb opened up, like a slit in a curtain.

I saw Clover standing in the other entranceway. She was sniffling but watching intently.

Dad, Dad, she said in my mind.

Don't worry, I said. *Stay still and close your eyes.*

The creature started to crawl into the opening of the orb. The swarm in my head was intercepting something. It wasn't quite words, but I could tell the orb was its ship, and that the creature was going to return home.

"We have to get outside," I yelled. "It's going to break through the roof!"

That didn't happen though.

Instead, a jolt of blue electricity surged up the orb thread from the wall socket. The lights started flickering. Clover and Iris screamed and ran outside. I started to follow them, but before we could make it out, there was a loud pop and all the lights shut off. Everything turned black.

I could sense something, either panic or resignation, coming from the creature. I opened a long cut on my calf scrambling out of the house. Iris and Clover were already in the yard.

"I guess the fuses blew," I said.

Iris smiled and guffawed. Clover was smiling too, but I didn't get why.

"We should move farther back," I said.

We don't have to. He can't leave, Clover said. *The vessel was only partially born. He'll have to stay with us!*

The air was cool outside, and the stars were shining brightly. We stood out in the yard for a while before the creature tumbled out of the house. It seemed Clover was right. The pink creature looked confused rolling around the wet grass. No one said anything, not even Clover.

I couldn't tell if it saw us, or even if it cared we were there. Maybe it didn't care about anything now. It inched away in a different direction, moving slowly toward the dark, open woods.

"Yes, leave, you asshole!" Iris finally said when it was almost out of sight. "I hope Dolan's ghost haunts you all the way to Mars!"

I guess it wasn't much of a surprise, but Iris and I didn't last much longer. We made it back to the city intact, but everything that had happened was too much for her. Or maybe we just weren't meant to be.

She moved out of her apartment a few weeks later, saying it smelled too much like Dolan. I never did learn if there was anything more going on there. Soon Iris left the city and flew across the country. She sent me one postcard with a picture of tanned bodies on the beach that said, "Wish you were here to oil me up!" but on the back she had written, "I know it isn't your fault, but that thing that killed Dolan is in your bloodstream. I can't fuck someone knowing there is an alien eye on the back of their neck. I hope you understand. Formerly yours, Iris."

I'm doing all right though. I'm not as angry as I used to be. When I get worked up, my head throbs, so I have to be calm and let things move through me. The eye on the back of my neck doesn't look too much bigger, but it's hard to tell. I wear a lot of turtlenecks.

Plus, I've got someone to take care of now. Little Clover, who likes to play Nintendo and makes us go out on the roof to watch the sky at night.

What happened to my second daddy? she asks me. *When's he coming back to take us away to a planet that isn't full of jerks?* She has more of the flesh in her than me, so I don't bother lying to her. She'd know. I say it probably died in those woods. Most likely it got mistaken for a deer by a hunter and shot, or else chewed up by wolves.

But Clover, I say, *even when we die, we never truly go away.*

I don't mean that hogwash about friends and family living on in our memories. I mean that creatures like Clover and me, those with the star-fallen flesh inside us, are not restrained by these bodies. When we die, even the worms and bugs that inspect our remains become touched. Our life force multiplies inside them, creating yet more vessels that crawl through the dark soil with new purpose. They spill out onto the green grass to scatter and grow and spread.

GETTING THERE NONETHELESS

They found the first one behind an abandoned barn. He was
tangled up in a mess of barbed wire and leaking opaque
purple liquid from holes in his stomach. Tim tried to call Tracy
but couldn't get reception. Byrd hit the thing in the face with a
stick. Charlotte screamed and snapped a few photos. All the man
could do was moan, moan, moan. Then his jaw got unhinged
from Byrd's stick.

"Hoorar? Ooorhar?" the man said.

They left him there and went back to the house to get Tracy.
Tim kept looking over his shoulder, but nothing burst through
the leaves.

It was a really spectacular July day in the country, so hot
that even breathing seemed to burn your insides. Clouds of
nearly invisible insects hovered everywhere. The four friends
were taking a two-week summer vacation in Charlotte's family's
cabin. Three months earlier, Charlotte had peed on a stick to
confirm she was pregnant. They'd all cleared up time to cele-
brate before real life really took over.

The reports of the disease were just starting when they'd
driven out of the city, but each time one came on, they'd hit
scan until they got music again.

"Tracy, we found one of those moaning dead guys!" Tim
shouted.

"He means *un*dead guys," Byrd said.

Tracy was tanning on the roof. She looked down at the upturned faces of her friends.

"I thought he was just sick at first and tried to help him, and he clawed my shoulder like an asshole!" Charlotte said.

"That's awful," Tracy said. "We need to lock the doors and search for weapons!"

"I wouldn't worry about it," Byrd said. "He was pretty trapped in that barbed wire."

"Well, let's get Charlotte to the hospital before she turns."

"Don't be dramatic, Tracy. It was a scratch, not a bite. Plus, I have this amazing balm made with aloe and goji berries that can, no joke, cure *anything*."

Tracy climbed down the ladder and went inside. Byrd was rubbing sunscreen up and down his arms.

"Tim and I can take care of him later. It'll be a bonding experience." Byrd swung an arm around Tim's neck and gave him a noogie.

Charlotte came out of the bathroom in a neon-green bikini with Band-Aids on her shoulder. "I thought we could take a dip in the lake. It's more like a pond I guess, but it has a zip line my dad strung up when we were kids. I know, I know. Hashtag tomboy, hashtag redneck. It's fun though!"

"That sounds nice," Tracy said uneasily.

"I was hoping to get some work done," Tim said. Tim had been insisting on working on his novel, or pretending to as far as Tracy could tell, even on vacation.

"Work in the shade, dummy," Byrd said.

Charlotte picked at her shoulder. "That asshole's fingers were disgusting. I'd like to think that even if I was undead, I'd practice some basic hygiene."

Tracy and Charlotte raced across the pond and pulled themselves onto the far dock.

"I'm going to get a little sun on my boobs now that we're away from those awful boys." Charlotte arched her back to slide off her top.

Tracy looked out the side of her eyes. Charlotte's nipples were red and enormous. Tracy wondered if babies had nipple preferences. If she ever decided to have a baby, would it find her nipples too small to suckle?

The sun was making Tracy sleepy. Bloated white clouds lumbered about overhead.

"I'd love to just live out here in nature, surrounded by trees and birds," Charlotte sighed.

"Why not do it?" Tracy said. "I'm glad my parents raised me with woods around."

Charlotte sat up. "Oh, I meant, like, rhetorically. I'm not raising my kid away from civilization to be a cultureless hillbilly. No offense."

Across the pond, Byrd and Tim were tossing a football around. Back in high school, Byrd had been the star quarterback, Charlotte was a cheerleader, and Tim had been the second-string punter—at least until he injured his knee junior year. Tracy didn't join the group until she started dating Tim in college, and she still felt like something of an outsider.

Charlotte drummed her belly and hummed a Beyoncé song. Tracy closed her eyes and tried to imagine the warmth of the sun sinking through her skin and cooking her evenly all the way through.

"I think the goal of life is more life," Charlotte said suddenly and philosophically. "When are you and Tim going to get started on that?"

"We haven't really talked about it." Tracy had always been told you would see anything you were thinking about in the clouds, but none of them looked like babies just then.

"When our mothers were young, you could just pop them out whenever. But with the cost of help and private schools, you really have to plan these days." Charlotte rolled over onto her stomach. Her scratched-up shoulder was a few inches from Tracy's face. Most of the Band-Aids had fallen off in the water. There was a shiny yellow sheen developing over the wound. A small dragonfly alighted on it, and Tracy shooed it away.

"Ah, listen to me," Charlotte said. "If I turn into one of those mommy bloggers who always blabbers mindlessly about her kid, promise me you'll shoot me in the face."

"Should I bring a knife or something?"

"This baby ought to do her," Byrd said, patting the shotgun.

They waved good-bye to Tracy and Charlotte, who were sipping margaritas—one virgin, one double tequila—out of jam jars on the porch.

"You boys be careful," Charlotte said.

"If that tequila's gone when we get back, I'm going to be pissed," Byrd said with a smile.

The road to the cabin was made of dusty gravel, and their feet crunched as they walked along. The sun was dipping behind the blue mountains, and nighttime creatures were awaking with chirps and growls. It was a little chilly, and Tim wished he had brought a jacket.

"This reminds me of the first time my dad took me hunting," Byrd said. "He didn't even tell me ahead of time, just woke me up at night and handed me face paint. I think I was eight years old. It was goose season. When we fired on them, hundreds flew into the air, and their wings and squawks were so loud I was too scared to be excited. In fact, I think I peed a little in my camo pants." Byrd swung the shotgun around in front of him. "Still, there's something about that first kill."

"I never went hunting," Tim said.

"Oh, right. I always forget your mother's a vegetarian."

"Vegan. But sometimes at the beach my father would secretly give me a crab hook. I tried to cook one with a lighter and threw up all over the pier. I guess that's pretty similar."

"Not at all, bro. Crabs don't scream."

They were coming around the bend near the old barn. Tim could hear a resigned groan above the crickets and hoots of owls. Byrd placed the shotgun gently in Tim's hands. "Here," he said in a fatherly tone. "I want you to do it."

Tim's father had managed a hedge fund and never understood Tim's love of sports. "Son," he'd said once, "you're in your prime education-maximizing period. What's your ROI if you get injured?" When Tim did get injured, snapping his ACL like an old rubber band, his father brought a stack of investment guides to his hospital bed.

Byrd and Tim walked off the road and onto the dirt path that led around the barn. Only the very last curve of the sun was left above the hills. Tim was surprised at how heavy a shotgun could be. He saw a pale bluish head rocking back and forth beyond the bushes. The man was standing in a pile of rotted firewood and barbed wire that he must have wrapped himself in trying to escape. His eyes were so sunken we could barely see them.

"He looks kind of sad," Tim said. "Maybe we should try to help him?"

"You can't help anyone who doesn't want to help themselves, especially when their brain has been eaten away by an undead plague."

As they came closer, the man started shaking. His jaw was unhinged, and a frothy yellow liquid dripped down his chin. He stretched one arm toward them. Flaps of skin were hanging off of it and shaking slightly in the wind.

"You have the safety on." Byrd reached over and pushed a button on the side of the gun.

The only time Tim had ever used a gun was at summer camp, and that was a .22 and soda cans. He pushed the butt into his shoulder like his counselor had taught him and squeezed the trigger.

The dead man's hand transformed into red confetti, and a large hole appeared in his upper chest. The shotgun popped out of Tim's hands.

"The brain!" Byrd yelled. Flecks of blood and blue skin covered his whole body. "You were supposed to shoot him in the fucking brain!"

The man was spinning now, digging himself deeper into the wires, one arm flapping around like a tetherball.

"Sorry, I told you I've never done this before."

Byrd bent down and picked up the shotgun. "Hey," he said. "Sorry I yelled. It's just that Charlotte bought me this polo for my birthday, and she already complains I don't wear it enough."

"I'm sorry."

"Nah, forget it. I'm just tense with the baby and everything." Byrd took the gun and fired the other shell into the head, which erupted backwards against the barn. "Let's go wash up and watch a movie with the gals."

Byrd and Charlotte were getting married in November, a few months before the baby was due. Byrd had borrowed enough money from his parents to buy a ring with two silver dolphins twirling around a giant diamond. Charlotte had always loved dolphins and had two of them leaping over a heart tattooed on her left thigh. Everyone knew Byrd and Charlotte were bound to tie the knot one of these days; the baby had only sped things up.

Tim wondered what it meant that he and Tracy were out here celebrating Charlotte and Byrd's baby and wedding. Did Byrd and Charlotte think they should get married too? Tim and Tracy had been dating for three years, but somehow marriage seemed like a stopping point. Tracy was still in law school, and Tim was draining his trust fund trying to finish his novel.

And what did Tracy think? Tim never knew anymore. They still had fun in public, but when their apartment door closed, it was nothing but fights or silence. Sometimes he got so angry he just wanted to scream at her. It felt like the two of them were just stumbling along, unsure of where they were going or why.

"Well, shit. Would you look at that?"

The four friends were eating penne arrabbiata on the porch. They all looked where Byrd was pointing. Out beyond the small vegetable garden, they saw a hunched-over man. He knocked over the chicken wire fence and slowly trudged through the small garden, emerging with tomato vines wrapped around his right leg.

"What the hell?" Byrd said with a mouth half-full of noodles. "Those were heirloom."

"Get inside!" Tracy yelled, jumping out of her seat.

"Hold on a sec," Byrd said. "We shouldn't have to have *our* meal ruined just because *he* failed to stay alive."

The man didn't seem to be paying any attention to his surroundings. He was moving in a general direction, but constantly bumping into the sides of trees, chairs, and other objects in the yard. He gave a loud groan, righted himself, and moved onward.

"Look, he's not even coming at us."

Indeed, the man's trajectory was past the house on the other side from the porch. The sight of him made Tracy shudder.

His skin was purple in the evening light. There were small red marks all over his legs, as if he'd been nipped by squirrels.

"Do you need any help?" Tracy called out.

The man didn't seem to register her words and stumbled out of view in his slow, sad gait.

The friends sat quietly for a bit, then resumed eating their food. Merle Haggard was playing on the portable speakers. Byrd screwed open another bottle of wine.

"I'd like to propose a toast," Byrd said. "To good friends, good eating, and no clients boring us with all their problems."

"Amen to that," Tracy said.

"And to the two of you," Tim said. "Soon to be three!"

Charlotte didn't say anything. She was slouched in her chair with sweat staining the upper half of her yellow blouse. Tracy thought she looked drunk, even though she hadn't had any wine.

"Do you need some water, Charlotte?" Tracy said.

Charlotte leaned forward and vomited blood across the picnic table.

Over the next few days they saw five more of them. They seemed like they had been normal people before the disease. Some had glasses and sun hats on. One was only a little kid, who kept bumping into the sliding glass doors of the porch. Tracy swatted at his face with a broom until he moved off through the woods. Another got her hand stuck in the crook of a split tree trunk and stayed there all evening, groaning. In the morning, Tim found a torn-off hand covered in ants.

Other than that, the undead just slowly walked on through. They didn't seem to have any place in particular to get to, but they were getting there nonetheless.

■ ■ ■

"We have to call a hospital, Byrd!" Tracy said. She was standing outside of Byrd and Charlotte's room. Tim was sitting on the couch, Googling information on zombism. He found a long list of symptoms on WebMD, but the treatments were all unsubstantiated or involved decapitation.

"Goddamnit, I said I'm taking care of it."

Loud thumps came from the room. Tracy frowned at Tim. The disease was spreading exponentially, and the whole state was overwhelmed. Even if the police came, Tim thought they'd probably just shoot Charlotte from the passenger window and drive off again.

A few minutes later, Byrd slid out of the bedroom door. He locked it behind him.

"Okay, under control," Byrd said. He gave Tracy and Tim a thin smile. His clothes were disheveled and his hair was matted with gray goo. "Hey, what do you guys want to do? Take a hike or a swim maybe?"

"I think we need to deal with this situation," Tracy said.

"I'm not going to be micromanaged on this, Tracy."

"Well, I think we should have a vote. Right, Tim?"

Byrd punched the wall several times.

"God fucking Christ shit!" he said. "She's tied up to the damn support beam! She isn't going anywhere. We are not taking a vote on whether Charlotte's head gets blown off or not!"

Tim was worried about Tracy. Byrd marched around the house like nothing was going on, but Tracy barely left the guest room. When she did, it was with a kitchen knife and wild eyes. At night, they could hear moans from the room next-door. Tracy would cry, and Tim didn't know what to do. She would grab him and kiss him and force him quickly inside her before he was even hard, crying the whole time.

Tracy tiptoed back into the room.

"Grab your bag and let's go!" she whispered.

"Huh?" Tim said, slowly opening his eyes. "I thought we were leaving on Saturday?"

"I stole Byrd's car keys. Do you want to get out of this death trap or not?"

Tim was sitting up now. He scratched his head and walked into the bathroom to urinate. "How will we get Charlotte in the car?" he said.

"That thing isn't Charlotte, and we aren't bringing it."

"But she's your BFF."

Tracy had to keep shushing Tim as they walked through the house.

"*Huffington Post* said it was safer in remote locations."

"Not if your remote location already has one growling in the bedroom next to yours!"

Tracy drove slowly up the road, hoping not to wake Byrd.

Tim reached over and fiddled with the radio. The only station that came on had a Christian preacher singing a hymn about the end times. Tracy pushed the rubber power button off.

The top of the driveway was blocked by a car crash.

"There's got to be a way around it," Tracy said. She turned on the high beams to get a better look. That's when she noticed the bodies in the car. She turned the headlights off. She started to cry, and after a minute, Tim put a hand on her neck and rubbed the soft hairs there. He stopped when he heard a dog barking.

"Oh my god, there's a dog trapped in there."

"Can dogs be zombies?" Tim said. He started to open the passenger door. The dog's barks got louder. They heard the sound of an oncoming car and loud whoops.

"What the hell is going on anymore?" Tracy said.

There were two loud blasts from sawed-off shotguns as a group of screaming men in hunting gear drove by. The bodies in the car started to thrash around. They seemed to be trapped in their seat belts.

"One more pass, boys!"

The tires screeched and roared by as three men braced in the back of a pickup truck let loose another volley of gunfire. All of the windows of the crashed cars erupted, and something soft and wet landed on the windshield of Byrd's car.

"Holy shit!" Tim said.

Tracy watched as the right side of the dog's face slid down the windshield, one large eye seeming to scan the length of her body.

She put the car in reverse and backed down the driveway.

The internet went down and three days later the TV. The landline had been giving them nothing but a monotone beep for over a week. Tracy took the radio into her and Tim's room and listened to it every night for news. Mostly they got static, but every two hours the hiss would dry up for one of two prerecorded announcements. The first urged calm and recommended various home treatments if licensed medical practitioners could not be reached. The second message urged calm and two bullets from no farther than twenty feet away to any victim's cerebral cortex.

Tim stumbled on Byrd in the hammock by the woodshed. He was swinging sadly with one foot on the ground.

"I thought there might be some canned goods in the shed."

"This was the first place." Byrd sniffled. He moved his legs for Tim to sit down.

"What?" Tim said.

"Sophomore year, when we all came up here for spring break instead of going to Florida with everyone else. When you guys were watching old slasher movies, Charlotte and I sneaked out here and drank a bottle of Ketel One. When she pulled her shirt off, her breasts looked like . . . Christ. What the fuck are we going to do, man?"

They sat there swinging. Even though he was a writer, or trying to be, Tim didn't know what to say. He tried to think about what his coach would tell them after a big loss. "Sometimes things look bad, and they might even be bad, but the important thing is to pick yourself up and get ready for the next play that life throws at you," he said.

Byrd cocked his head at Tim. The wind was warm and rattled the ripe leaves above their heads. In the distance, something moaned.

"What in the shit fuck does that mean?"

"Hi, Tracy."

"Oh god!" Tracy jumped back against the laundry machine. She had been searching for a flashlight since the power had blinked off that morning.

"Do you ever wonder what love is?" Byrd said. He had dark bags under his eyes, and his clothes were dirty and filled with rips and holes.

"I have a knife," Tracy said.

"Is love doing whatever you can do to synergize with someone? Is it giving up your own self to be what they need you to be?" Byrd was looking past Tracy at the rows of chemicals and tools. His shoulders were slumped, and he scratched at his neck with one long fingernail. "Coach always said love was sacrifice. He was talking about football, but is it the same thing with people?"

Tracy felt the terrible sadness that had been living in her for weeks rise up into her face. "I don't know, Byrd," she said. "I don't know anything anymore."

Byrd jiggled the doorknob and shouted, "Hey, the door is locked."

Tim opened the door, then sat back on the bed with Tracy.

Byrd was wearing a dress shirt and a tie, and his blond hair was greased up and combed back. He looked as if he hadn't slept in days. His skin was covered in scabs.

Tracy held on to Tim's hand so hard her nails cut little semi-circles into his palm.

"Guys, I just want you to know what amazing friends you've been and how much I've treasured life's journey with you, even though the journey turned on to a burning road of shit. I always thought of you like a little brother, Tim. Tracy, I know Charlotte was going to surprise you later by asking you to be her maid of honor. Isn't it crazy we've known each other for twelve years?"

He stayed at the door and gulped in his throat. Tim and Tracy didn't say anything.

"Tim, buddy, I'm sorry I broke the bro code and slept with Tracy. You two are welcome to stay here as long as you can. Maybe you can even build a life together while everything else is falling apart. Just remember that love is the key."

Byrd surveyed them for one last time, sniffled, and closed the door.

"What?" Tim shouted.

"Oh my god," Tracy said. "What is he going to do?"

"You slept with Byrd?"

"Tim, we have to stop him." Tracy jumped up and headed for the door. They could hear thumping and sporadic moans from the room next door.

"When did this happen?"

"I don't know. He was so sad. It just happened."

"Jesus Christ," Tim said. He lay back on the bed. "My best fucking friend."

"This isn't the time, Tim!"

But Tim stayed there on the bed, moaning. Tracy stayed with him. They listened to a door opening and the sounds of two people shuffling down the hall and out into the lush woods.

The undead continued to come and go. Some stumbled to the north and others ambled toward the south. Tracy thought they were different ones each time, until she saw the man who'd ripped up their garden crawling across the backyard. He was missing a foot, part of his rib cage, and both eyes, but the dried-up tomato vines were still wrapped around his leg.

Tim came into the living room holding a dusty box.

"Hey, I found this jigsaw puzzle."

Tracy was sitting on one of the only chairs that hadn't been used to reinforce the doors. She had the shotgun between the chair legs.

"That's great, Tim. Productive."

"Look you don't have to be sarcastic," Tim said. "I'm just trying to be proactive."

Tracy saw something at the edge of the woods and jumped for the gun, but it was only a baby deer. Was it a zombie baby deer? She sat back down and looked at Tim. He looked so angry and sad, but she didn't know what to say. They had no electricity, no home they could return to, and only half a grocery bag of food left. She hadn't done anything she'd wanted to do in life. She hadn't gotten her JD, hadn't learned ballroom dancing, and never got to live in Venice. For all she knew, Venice didn't even exist anymore. She hadn't even finished *War and Peace* yet for Christ's sake.

"Fuck it," Tim said after a while. "I'm going to go root through the storage room in the basement."

"No, wait," she said, forcing a smile. "I'll come with you. Maybe we can find a flare gun or something."

A week later, while searching the forest's edge for kindling, Tim was injured when Byrd, Charlotte, and a crawling, half-formed blue fetus leapt out from behind a sycamore tree, grappled him to the ground, and sunk in their teeth.

Tracy found Tim crawling toward the front porch, bleeding and moaning. She screamed and locked the door. Tim heaved his body against the wood. Tracy watched through the peephole and cried for a long time.

She poured a glass of wine she had distilled from wild blackberries, sat down, and closed her eyes. She could still hear Tim's muffled thumps. Her hands were shaking, and some of the wine in her glass spilled down her arm. It dried there in dark red streaks.

Tracy thought about her life with Tim. They had met, drunk, at a party during her first weekend as a college freshman. He had fallen asleep on top of her two minutes into sex, and she could barely breathe. His warm body was comforting though. Second semester they had the same sociology class, and he asked her out, and she thought he seemed sweet. Things snowballed along in the way they do. She had even thought they might get married since they'd been together for so long, and she didn't know what else to do.

Tim had always been nice to her, always buying her little bundles of flowers that died in a day or two. She felt she had never been as nice to him. She liked to spend her time by herself, and he always seemed angry about how often she couldn't fit him in to her schedule. Tim was always angry about so many things, from his failed sports career to his nonexistent writing career.

If she ignored Tim, maybe he would crawl away and go where all the other undead people were going. Maybe that would be the place where he could be happy.

For the next five mornings, Tracy awoke to Tim's thumps. She realized he was never going to go away. He was going to keep thumping against the wood, compelled by some brainless inertia, until he turned into mush on the doorstep.

The sun was shining angrily through a hole in the curtain. After eating the last of the oatmeal, she sneaked out the side door and went to the shed. She grabbed the largest weapon she could lift and walked back to the front porch.

Tim felt pain. Saw Tracy and Tracy was sad. Tracy was sad and causing pain to Tim. Causing pain with sharp metal thing.

Tim held up hand. Tracy brought down metal thing and hand fell off. Held up other hand. Same thing.

Water came out Tracy's eyes.

"Gwah?" Tim said.

Tim didn't understand. Tim didn't understand pain or sadness. Never understood whole life. Tim thought pain and sadness would never stop. Hoped stop all time. Hurt all over and wanting to hurt other things. Always like this. Every day he remember. Why? Angry at sad and pain. On and on.

"Klluuuuurggg," Tim said. "Traggeee! Gwah? Gwah? Gwaahh?"

ACKNOWLEDGMENTS

$\mathbf{M}$any thanks to:

My friends and fellow writers who read drafts of these stories, especially Adrian Van Young, James Yeh, John Dermot Woods, Chloé Cooper Jones, and Adam Wilson.

All the professors and mentors who encouraged me, especially Sam Lipsyte, Alan Ziegler, Ben Marcus, Rebecca Curtis, Maxine Clair, David McAleavey, Rob Spillman, and Diane Williams.

My *Gigantic* people.

Halimah Marcus, Andy Hunter, and Electric Literature.

Friends who provided advice or support, including Ann DeWitt, Rozalia Jovanovic, Isaac Fitzgerald, Ryan Britt, Benjamin Samuel, Will Chancellor, Catherine Foulkrod, and Justin Taylor.

Internet literary friends. You are real to me.

My brother, my mother, and my father.

The Millay Colony, the Lower Manhattan Cultural Council, and the Virginia Center for the Creative Arts for much needed space and time.

Every magazine, journal, or site that published my work over the years.

Michelle Brower, my agent, who fought to find my work a home.

Anitra Budd, my fantastic editor, as well as Chris Fischbach, Caroline Casey, Molly Fuller, Amelia Foster, and everyone else at Coffee House for seeing something in these odd little stories.

Most of all Nadxieli Nieto for counsel, support, design, and everything else.

And, of course, last but never least—I couldn't forget—thanks are due to you, you vile, luminescent animal, sitting there with this book in your gnarled and sculpted hands.

A NOTE ON THE TYPE

This work has been set in Berdych, a typeface named after Antun Berdych, who was a prominent typesetter and printer in the first half of the seventeenth century. The typeface was originally designed as a stunted, incongruous font, with the kerning between the glyphs inconsistent and the vowels improperly rounded. The typeface was given its name by rival typesetter Milos Heyduk on the occasion of Berdych's death in April of 1657. Heyduk designed the typeface to cause strain in the eyes while reading and to impart a lingering ocular discomfort throughout the day.

Heyduk and Berdych were neighbors as children, both born into long lines of carriage makers in the southern Czech town of Pisek. Local legend says both boys pined after little Rayna Richta, the last daughter of lingering Hussite nobility. As children, they played the usual games of rocks and sticks in the dusty streets together. Berdych always knocked the rock farthest and broke the stick quickest, while the clumsier and more portly Heyduk would trip and fall into the dusty street. "Come Milos," Antun would say, "You're rolling in the dirt like a filthy piglet." Little Rayna would giggle with glee.

It was expected that both boys would follow in their wood-shaping fathers' footsteps, but young Antun and Milos became embroiled in the typesetting heyday of the early 1600s. Both decided to leave Pisek to seek their fortunes: Berdych to Paris,

Heyduk to Antwerp, Cologne, and then Berlin. Both men found some degree of success, but it was Berdych's early seventeenth-century print series of French erotica commissioned by the Duke of Lorraine that propelled him to instant stardom in the close-knit world of typesetting. Berdych rode his success by designing a startling series of elegant yet salacious typefaces—the glyphs allegedly fashioned after the curves of his various mistresses—that caused disquiet and scandal among high society.

For his part, Heyduk developed a line of competent, stout typefaces that found an acceptable following among German accountants. After two decades in Berlin, Heyduk returned to Pisek with his modest savings and attempted to kindle a romance with Rayna Richta, whose first husband had died at the infamous Battle of White Mountain in the early days of the Thirty Years' War. Heyduk set up his shop on a lonely street in the south side of Pisek and slowly wooed the widow Rayna for many years, until—when her savings had run dry and her looks had faded in the mirror—she consented to marry again. The Heyduks' marriage progressed satisfactorily for a decade until 1642, when Antun Berdych, beginning to tire of the overwhelming life of Parisian high society, returned to Pisek and set up his famed Golden Drips printing shop.

The homecoming of the handsome and now famous typesetter, complete with his by all accounts beautiful Parisian bride, Stephanie née Verdurin, caused something of a stir in Pisek. The couple arrived by way of the rivers Vltava and Otava on a royal barge on loan from the King of Bohemia and Holy Roman Emperor himself, Ferdinand III. The citizens were overjoyed to have their most famous son returned. Town records indicate the homecoming celebration lasted for sixty-eight hours and involved the accidental deaths of at least two townspeople.

Milos Heyduk watched with barely contained venom as Berdych's Golden Drips shop was erected across the street from his own modest shop. Every day, Heyduk glared at the stream of prominent clients from Prague and Vienna approaching Berdych's shop while his own stayed dim and empty. At night he watched Berdych strolling past his office window with his beautiful wife, whose features so contrasted with the withered faces of Rayna and himself. Over the years, these images turned Heyduk into a foul and bitter man. He would toss rocks at dogs, taunt children that approached his shop, and fight with his wife so loudly the neighbors were kept up long into the night.

For either revenge or refuge, Rayna began an affair. When Heyduk learned of the cuckoldry, he smothered her to death in their bed with the straw-filled sack that served as their pillow. The police found him the next day, sleeping soundly with Rayna's body knocked onto the floor. Although it is commonly believed that it was Antun Berdych who seduced Rayna and coaxed her into having the affair that led to the grisly nighttime murder, this is apocryphal. In truth, the Berdych that Rayna conducted an affair with was a local cobbler of no relation.

Heyduk was incarcerated for several decades. During this time, Antun Berdych developed the incurable case of consumption from which he eventually perished. Upon the news of his rival's death, Heyduk quickly began designing the Berdych typeface on smuggled paper in the corner of his prison cell. Upon his release, Heyduk employed the unpleasant typeface almost exclusively. He printed it on newsletters and flyers that he tacked on every wooden door in Pisek. The typeface soon became famous for its sordid origin and its attachment to the celebrated Berdych. In a diary entry near the date of his death, Heyduk remarks, "Although I will soon be snatched away by my maker, I comfort myself with the knowledge that Antun, that horse's ass, will be forever linked with discomfort and ugliness."

Over the centuries, various typesetters have fixed the irregularities in the Berdych typeface and reshaped many of the serifs to come into line with Berdych's own manuscripts. Today it is widely regarded as one of the most royal and elegant typefaces and enjoys a dedicated following in scholarly circles. Heyduk's original designs are said to still be held in the basement of the Pisek Public Library. The visiting hours are 10 a.m. to 2 p.m. on weekdays.

The text of *Upright Beasts* is set in Weiss.
Composition by Bookmobile Design & Digital
Publisher Services, Minneapolis, Minnesota.